Hidden in the Heart

Hidden in
the Heart

Beth Andrews

ROBERT HALE · LONDON

© Beth Andrews 2006
First published in Great Britain 2006

ISBN-10: 0-7090-8109-X
ISBN-13: 978-0-7090-8109-8

Robert Hale Limited
Clerkenwell House
Clerkenwell Green
London EC1R 0HT

2 4 6 8 10 9 7 5 3 1

Typeset in 11½/17pt New Century Schoolbook
by Derek Doyle & Associates, Shaw Heath
Printed in Great Britain by St Edmundsbury Press
Bury St Edmunds, Suffolk
Bound by Woolnough Bookbinding Limited

I,
the author of the following opus,
do hereby dedicate
this poor bagatelle
to Raymond and Mebane
for your support and encouragement
to starving artists
of the romantic kind
(Notably myself)

CHAPTER ONE

AN AWKWARD BUSINESS

'Pink satin! It must be pink satin – with cocquelicot ribbons.'

Louisa's cheeks were alarmingly hectic, her mouth a thin line of mutinous determination. It was plain to Lydia that, if they were not careful, one of her sister's famous tantrums was about to break over them.

'Muslin is less expensive,' Mama suggested hesitantly, 'and white is quite the thing for a young girl in her first season.'

'Oh Mama!' Louisa wailed. 'It will be but too shabby. I shall look a veritable pauper.'

'We are not precisely wealthy, my dear,' Mrs Bramwell reminded her eldest daughter.

'Punting on River Tick,' Lydia added, 'in a decidedly leaky vessel.'

'For Heaven's sake, mind your tongue, Lydia!' Her mother pressed a hand to her forehead in exasperation. 'Such cant terms are not at all the thing, and never used by persons with the least pretension to gentility.'

Louisa sniffed loudly. 'Lydia cannot open her mouth without something vulgar coming out of it.'

'I am sure I do not sound half so vulgar as you will look in that pink satin horror you wish to wear,' Lydia protested. 'People will take you for some dreadful creature from the stage.'

Louisa's face turned a shade remarkably like that of the dress she so desired. 'Why you stupid little—'

'Enough!' Mrs Bramwell's unusually stern tones halted her before anything too shocking could issue from her lips. 'The pair of you will drive me to bedlam yet! My nerves cannot endure any more of your quarrels.'

'What does Lydia know of fashion, in any case?' Louisa hunched up a delicately curved shoulder. 'I am sure the only colour she cares for is blue – as her stockings must be.'

'It would do you no harm to read something more edifying than *La Belle Assemblée*,' Lydia retorted, stung by the condescending accusation.

She glared at her elder sister, who was twirling about in front of the gilded mirror in their small parlour. Louisa, she considered, was a pretty ninnyhammer. Blue eyes, pink cheeks and golden hair she had in abundance. However, beneath the gold was a mind which never bothered about anything but fashion and frivolity.

On the other hand, perhaps she *was* guilty of envy where her sister was concerned. The family was generally considered to be very good-looking, but Lydia knew herself to be the plainest of them. Her hair was mouse-coloured rather than golden; her *retroussé* nose might be considered charming by some but was scarcely out of the common way. And as for her grey eyes, if they sparkled at all, it was usually with contempt at the follies of those around her.

'You should not speak so to your sister, Lydia,' Mrs Bramwell interrupted her thoughts. 'Louisa knows what she is about. Book-learning is all very well, but it is of little use in catching a husband.'

'But suppose,' Lydia countered mischievously, 'that one does not want a husband?'

'It is as well if *you* do not,' Louisa answered her. 'You would have a hard enough task getting one!'

'I see no ring on *your* finger yet,' Lydia answered back, poking her tongue out at her for good measure.

Louisa returned the favour, adding, 'I'll have a rich husband by the time I return from London. You may be sure of that.'

'It is essential that you marry well, dearest,' Mrs Bramwell said – somewhat grimly, it seemed to Lydia. 'How else are we to restore the family fortunes?'

Lydia frowned at this. 'I think you must be mistaken, Mama.'

'I assure you, Lydia, I am not! Louisa must make an advantageous match. And,' she conceded, eyeing her eldest child indulgently, 'I am convinced that, with her looks, she cannot help but achieve her goal.'

'So I shall!' Louisa asserted confidently.

'That was not what I meant,' Lydia explained.

'Then what *did* you mean, brat?' Louisa snapped.

'It is just that you said we must *restore* the family's fortunes.' Lydia shook her head. 'That implies that we at one time had a fortune to be restored. If anyone in our family ever had any wealth, I certainly never heard of it.'

It was Mrs Bramwell's turn now to frown. Her daughter's practical observation clearly did not sit well with one whose ambition was to attain social distinction for her daughters, even if she could not procure as much for herself. The Bramwells were quite a respectable family, after all, and looked up to in the village as some of its most ancient inhabitants. There had been Bramwells at Laburnum Lodge for as long as anyone could remember. If they had little wealth, they had a certain degree of distinction. The present occupant was a solicitor, and of considerable standing in his small community. However, this was not enough to satisfy the mistress of the house. Her husband might be content with an obscure and quiet life in the country, but she was determined that her children should not be allowed to decline into mere bumpkins.

Mrs Bramwell had a cousin in London with her own pretensions, who had graciously consented to assist Louisa with her presentation into polite society. For this long-anticipated event, Mrs Bramwell had been saving and planning many years. Now at last the time had come. Louisa was almost nineteen. Who could tell how long it might take for her to attach an eligible gentleman? Time, as all women knew, was not their friend in such matters. Better to strike while youth and beauty still had power to entice those who looked no deeper than the surface of things.

Lydia could not see the thoughts jostling about in her mother's head, but she had wits enough to guess most of them. However, she had little expectation of any great match for her sister. Wealthy and influential men, she considered, rarely allied themselves to penniless nobodies from the country – however pretty they might be.

Still, she looked forward to visiting London – a place she had heard much about but never seen. It would be quite an adventure. Alas, for her it was not to be.

The very next day, a letter arrived. This was an event unusual enough to capture Lydia's interest. She observed her father pay the charge before carrying the folded and sealed paper into the parlour to examine its contents, and immediately followed him to see what she might learn.

'Who is it from, Papa?' Louisa was quite as curious as Lydia. They rarely received mail. When they did, papa had been known to mumble words which his children did not comprehend but which surely were not kindly. Without a frank, one had liefer not hear from one's relations rather than having to pay for the privilege of reading their almost illegible prose.

'Is it from my sister in Sussex?' Mrs Bramwell asked her husband.

'So it seems.'

Lydia eyed both her parents suspiciously. Papa's head was bent over the missive, so that she could perceive how the hair on his crown was noticeably thinner than that which fell across his brow. His brow was furrowed now in the effort of concentration and his lips compressed.

'Is it what we have been waiting for?' his wife persisted.

'It is what *you* have been waiting for, my dear,' her husband answered wryly. 'I, like Pilate, am eager to wash my hands of this awkward business.'

'What awkward business?' Lydia demanded before Louisa could ask the same question.

'Lydia, my dear,' Mrs Bramwell hesitated a trifle, 'you know that our poor resources will be stretched to their absolute limit by Louisa's presentation.'

'I am amazed that they can stretch as far,' her youngest daughter admitted bluntly.

'Indeed.' Mama seemed strangely pleased, rather than pained by her perspicacity. 'You do understand, don't you, dearest child?'

Lydia stiffened at once. Mama never referred to her as her 'dearest child' unless she was about to do or say something particularly unpleasant. On all other occasions, it was plain that Louisa was her favourite – just as Lydia knew herself to be papa's favourite child. Not that either of her parents would have admitted as much, of course.

'What is it, Mama? What is wrong?'

'Wrong?' Mrs Bramwell giggled nervously, fingering her lace collar and looking in every direction at once, save in the direction of her daughter. 'Nothing is wrong, dearest. But you must see that, in the circumstances, it is impossible for all of us to go up to London.'

'Lydia is not coming with us?' Louisa squealed with malicious delight. 'Oh, that is too bad!'

'Try, if you can, to stifle your grief, Louisa,' Lydia answered.

'I'm afraid it is a matter of strict economy,' Papa said, his tone displaying more real dismay at the prospect.

'That I can well believe,' Lydia admitted.

'I am sure you do not mind,' Mama said reassuringly. 'You do not care so much for balls and parties as Louisa does.'

'True, true,' papa put in, with a proud glance at his youngest. 'You have a head on your shoulders, my dear.'

'And what have I, Papa?' Louisa demanded. 'A cabbage?'

'A cabbage might be more to the purpose,' Lydia said sweetly, 'in our impecunious state. At least it would be edible. And most cabbages, I warrant, would have more sense.'

'Now do not start quarrelling again, girls,' their mother said with weary perseverance.

'Indeed I envy you, Lydia.' There could be no doubt of Mr Bramwell's sincerity. 'I should much prefer the pleasures of Sussex to the noise and nothingness of London.'

'I am to stay with Aunt Camilla?'

'She has graciously offered to take you in for the next eight weeks,' Mrs Bramwell elucidated.

'Offered!' Mr Bramwell's snort indicated that this was not precisely the way he understood the matter. Lydia easily – and quite correctly – inferred that the idea had been entirely her mother's, and that it had taken a great deal of persuasion before her aunt would consent.

'Poor Lydia!' Louisa shook her head in mock sympathy. 'But when I am married,' she added with conscious superiority, 'you shall often visit me in my London house.'

'Not *very* often,' Lydia muttered grimly, only just managing to refrain from reminding her that both her marriage and her London house existed only in her imagination.

'Perhaps my sister may be able to arrange a brief visit to Brighton,' Mrs Bramwell suggested.

'Brighton!' Louisa was not so elated at this. Brighton was the most fashionable resort for sea bathing, and a haunt of the Prince Regent himself.

'That *would* be pleasant,' Lydia said, enjoying a momentary elevation which her father promptly brought down to earth.

'Most unlikely, I should think,' Mr Bramwell observed to his wife. 'Your sister is not precisely plump in the pocket herself, my dear, and can scarcely afford such extravagance.'

'Poor Lydia!' Louisa repeated, her good humour restored.

It was a disappointment, to be sure, but Lydia was determined that it should not oppress her spirits. She was young enough still to find any change of place an adventure and any new acquaintance interesting.

London might boast a myriad of attractions, but beyond the circulating libraries and Ackerman's Repository, there was little to regret in not journeying thither. And who could tell what might await her in Sussex?

She could not recall meeting her mother's half-sister, Camilla. Although she was, in fact, mama's nearest relation, they had never been very close and seemed perfectly content not to see each other more than once in a decade.

They were quite different in age, of course. Their mother, Agnes, had the felicity of being twice married: first to Mr Thomson, which union had produced Mama, and, upon that gentleman's demise, the enterprising Agnes had married Mr Denton, a much older man. Camilla was the child of this second marriage, and had been born when her sister was already a strapping girl of thirteen.

Miss Thomson became Mrs Bramwell only five years later, and had moved to a different part of the country near London. Agnes passed away when her second daughter was a child of nine years; Mr Denton, now much stricken in years, followed her to the next world ten years later. Camilla inherited his estate, which was not large. It included her small cottage in the village of Diddlington near the banks of the Ouse, and an income sufficient to live comfortably but not with any pretension to luxury or profligacy.

Though she had passed thirty summers, Camilla Denton remained unwed. This, more than anything else that she knew of her aunt, made Lydia uneasy. Why had her aunt never married? Was she a bitter and mean-spirited old maid?

She hoped that her aunt would prove to be amiable, though she was doubtful of the possibility. Someone so stricken in years was more liable to be crotchety and cross, she surmised.

With a sigh, she lay her head upon her pillow and fell asleep, content to let the day's trouble be sufficient.

CHAPTER TWO

A PERILOUS JOURNEY

If adventure was what Lydia sought, the journey from London via the black and maroon Royal Mail coach provided an ample portion. Papa and mama could not afford the most expensive seat, and so she found herself perched precariously atop the roof, spending most of the journey clinging to a conveniently placed rail as they lurched and lunged their way along the roads of the south-east of England.

She had eaten a hearty meal before the coach departed, since there was no guarantee of further sustenance until the end of her journey. With strict instructions not to hob-nob with her fellow passengers, there was little to do but to observe them in stolid silence.

Beside her was an elderly dame whose countenance was so criss-crossed by fine wrinkles that it appeared like some fantastic map of the streets of London, with her nose rising up in the middle like the dome of St Paul's. Several times, when rounding a particularly sharp bend in the road, she had clutched at Lydia to save herself from tumbling off the swaying vehicle. Other than that, she betrayed no interest in her companion.

Across from them were two gentlemen at the rear. One was a rotund fellow with a balding pate and unusually small ears. The other appeared somewhat cadaverous, with large dark eyes and a pronounced beak which would have put Wellington's to shame. They were both of advanced years – fifty at least – and were generally too preoccupied with keeping themselves in their seats to give Lydia more than a smile or a wink of encouragement. In her mind, they became simply 'Nose' and 'Ears'.

On those occasions when the pace of the coach slowed or they were on a smooth stretch of road, she caught snatches of their conversation. They were both patrons of the theatre, and for several miles carried on a spirited debate over the rival merits of Kean and Kemble. Nose, it seemed, was personally acquainted with both of those illustrious thespians, and regaled the suitably awed Ears with anecdotes of life on the stage which Lydia suspected were completely fictitious.

'There is such nobility,' Ears argued at one point, 'in Mr Kemble's manner.'

'Well,' Nose commented with some contempt, 'every dog has his day, but I fear that Kemble's is all but over. Had you seen Kean in his first appearance as Shylock. . . .'

'Were you there?' Ears's eyes grew round as the coach wheels.

'Of course I was.' Nose seemed insulted at the suggestion

that he might have been absent from such a momentous occasion. 'Indeed, he was most grateful for my assistance. He gave me this.'

Here he paused to produce a silver-gilt watch at the end of an ornate chain. Lydia's gaze travelled to his pointing finger and she could just make out what appeared to be a pair of grotesquely carved faces engraved upon it. Very theatrical, she considered with distaste. Ears was much more impressed.

'By Jove!' he cried. 'You certainly have moved in exalted circles, sir.'

Nose preened himself and almost simpered in his pleasure at having excited such admiration. However, what he said in reply was lost to Lydia, as a passing phaeton almost ran them off the road at that very moment. Nose and Ears shouted a few choice words at the offending Jehu, and even Miss Map (as Lydia now thought of the old crone beside her) was roused to mutter something less than complimentary. Lydia's attention wandered, and it was several minutes before she picked up the thread of their conversation, which now led in a different direction.

'And your sister also appeared with Kean?' Ears was asking.

'Yes indeed.' Nose nodded vigorously. 'She was an exceptionally gifted actress, but never received the fame she deserved. Then, of course, she married Mr Cha—'

Once again their coze was interrupted – this time by the guard's ear-splitting blast upon the yard of tin, which startled Lydia herself and occasioned more complaints from her fellow travellers.

Lydia did not join in their protests, being too preoccupied with shifting her chip straw bonnet, which had listed alarmingly to port. Had she been the heroine in one of the latest romance novels which Louisa so loved, she reflected, she would assuredly have tumbled off the Mail and into the arms of a handsome nobleman. He would have spirited her off to his castle and sought to steal her virtue. What this actually would entail, she was not sure. Romances tended to be somewhat vague on that point. Inevitably, of course, her lively wit and manifold charms would have soothed the savage breast of the profligate duke or viscount and he would have begged for her hand in marriage.

However, as this was not a novel, nothing more alarming occurred. In fact, they had already arrived at Lewes. Here Lydia descended from the conveyance with an inward sigh of relief. She was glad that she would be spared any further discomfort or dangers – especially since the sky was darkening ominously, indicating an impending shower of rain which boded ill for the three remaining occupants of the coach's rooftop.

She hoped that Aunt Camilla was already there to meet her. The inn was respectable-looking, but she did not relish the thought of waiting about like a servant.

She could hear the cries of the hostlers as they hurried to change horses, and the general hubbub of activity as passengers scrambled for a bite of food before the coach departed once more. Fortunately, she had not been there five minutes before an elderly man came up to her, bowed hesitantly, and asked, 'Be you Miss Bramwell?'

Lydia nodded, eyeing him appraisingly.

'My name's Flitt, miss. Come this way, if you please,' he instructed her, turning toward the inn yard once more. 'I'll take you to your aunt.'

Timidity was foreign to Lydia's nature, but she did own to a slight *frisson* of apprehension as they approached the antiquated carriage which stood to one side, away from the frantic bustle surrounding the Mail.

As she drew nearer, the carriage door, with its faded paint, opened and out stepped a lady who was as different from the aged termagant of Lydia's imagination as a rose is from a thistle.

She had supposed that Aunt Camilla would look much like Mama. She was mistaken. Where her mother was short and plump, this lady was tall and willow-thin. Though her clothes were not in the latest fashion, she wore them with an air which lent a touch of elegance. Her face was a pale oval, with dark hair peeping from beneath her poke bonnet and large blue eyes that looked fearfully out at the world. Her lips were caught between her pearl-white teeth at the moment, but Lydia did not doubt that they were as delightful as the rest of her countenance. She was, in fact a beauty. Who would have thought it?

'Aunt Camilla?' Lydia spoke tentatively, considering that this might, in fact, be someone else who had been sent to collect her.

'Dearest Lydia!' the lady cried, stepping down to embrace her. 'Well! This is a happy occasion.'

'You are much prettier than I expected,' Lydia said with her usual candour.

21

Her aunt blushed and looked away. It seemed she was not accustomed to receiving compliments, even from her relations.

'But where is your maid?' she stammered, casting her gaze around the inn yard.

'I have none.'

The big blue eyes grew even larger.

'No maid!' Aunt Camilla was scandalized. 'What can your mother have been thinking? You are far too young to travel alone! I am astonished.'

In vain did Lydia attempt to explain that it was impossible for her parents to afford to pay the expense of sending a maid with their daughter. Her protests that she was a sensible girl fell on ears which refused to hear. It simply was inconceivable to the older woman that any girl of seventeen could be let loose on her own to traipse about the English countryside without doing irreparable damage to her reputation and very likely producing a national calamity.

'It is difficult to imagine,' Lydia said at last, 'what harm was likely to come to me on the common stage between London and Lewes.'

'You do not know the wickedness in this world, dear child,' Aunt Camilla commented.

Her dramatic utterance led Lydia to believe that she had been reading Mr Walpole or Mrs Radcliffe. Further conversation only confirmed this suspicion. Her aunt had a strong romantic tendency which her niece did not possess. At the same time, it seemed to Lydia that she was inordinately shy and retiring. After her initial homily on the danger which travel posed to innocent young females, she subsided into an uncomfortable silence, apparently at a loss for anything else to say.

'This is a very fine carriage,' Lydia said at last.

'Oh yes!' Camilla seemed relieved to find some topic of conversation. 'Mrs Wardle-Penfield was very generous to suggest that I might have the use of it.'

'It is not your own, then?' Lydia was surprised.

'Oh, no!' Her aunt was shocked at the suggestion. 'I cannot afford the expense of keeping a carriage. Besides, there is no purpose in keeping one. I live at the edge of the village, and everything needful is easily got to on foot.'

'Mrs Wardle-Penfield is a friend of yours?' Lydia enquired.

'Well . . .' Aunt Camilla chose her words carefully. 'She is a neighbour, and one of the – the pillars of Diddlington society.'

A little more coaxing and Lydia deduced that the lady in question was a managing female who had practically bullied her aunt into using her carriage so that the generous bounty of Mrs Wardle-Penfield could be trumpeted with perfect truth to all the surrounding country-side.

'It was most kind of her,' Lydia commented.

'Oh, she is always ready to offer help to those in need,' Camilla said, rather too quickly.

'No doubt she is well known in the village.'

'Indeed she is,' Camilla said emphatically, giving the impression that the woman could empty the high street by her mere presence there.

By the time they reached her aunt's house, Lydia's imagination had formed a fair portrait of her aunt's world. Her acquaintance comprised perhaps two dozen families. Beyond that, there were the servants and tradesmen, the vicar and the apothecary, and their attendant children and relations. London was a place which everyone knew of, but few had actually seen. All was quiet and uneventful.

Still, Lydia looked forward to meeting these various inhabitants of Diddlington, and felt perfectly satisfied with her lot. Louisa's giddy round of parties and her determined efforts to climb the Jacob's Ladder of society would not have pleased her half as well, nor would a rented house in London have been so inviting.

Aunt Camilla's cottage, while not precisely a commodious residence, was more than adequate for a spinster and her niece, with three very comfortable bedchambers. Two of these, of course, were scarcely ever occupied. There was a large parlour, which received plenty of light through two south-facing windows, and a small but neat kitchen. Her aunt boasted only two servants: a nearsighted housekeeper, Mrs Plumpton, and Charity, a maid of all work who did not live in but divided her duties between Aunt Camilla and Mrs Isherwood on the next street.

Lydia's bed was soft and warm, and most conducive to a night of uninterrupted sleep. She was certainly much better off where she was. If it offered no excitement, at least her memories of her brief season here were likely to be pleasant ones. No tread of violence could disturb this tranquil English idyll.

CHAPTER THREE

COUNTRY PLEASURES

Lydia was one who generally arose early in the morning. This was just as well, as she soon found that country hours were different from those in town and in the village of Shepperton, just on the edge of London, where her family resided. 'Early to bed and early to rise' was the maxim here.

By nine o'clock the next morning, she had breakfasted and dressed with the help of her aunt's maid. She then accompanied Aunt Camilla on a promenade along the high street. This, it seemed, was a ritual which all the most prominent citizens followed.

Lydia counted some twenty pedestrians as they made their way toward the haberdashery where her aunt meant to purchase some ribbons to trim a hat which wanted that special something to make it stand out among the *chapeaux* of her acquaintance. Twenty persons could be considered a crowd on the streets of Diddlington, Lydia supposed.

However, her aunt was eager to assure her that the town was rising in prominence these days. This was due to its favourable location on the banks of the Ouse between Piddinghoe and Tarring Neville. With easy access to both Lewes and Brighton for the popular races, the Golden Cockerel Inn had become quite the fashionable place for gentlemen to deposit those ladybirds whose plumage might be too colourful and attract unwanted attention in the larger towns. Aunt Camilla did not, of course, put things quite so crudely to her young charge. Unfortunately, Lydia was perfectly capable of gleaning as much with very little effort.

Still, on this occasion, the only persons they encountered were all very well known to Camilla. Jeremiah Berwick, the farrier, nodded and smiled a greeting, and several other gentlemen doffed their hats and gave an appreciative glance at her aunt's trim figure.

They entered the haberdasher's, which was actually quite large and well stocked for a country establishment, and soon found the ribbons which they sought – in a shade of blue to match her aunt's eyes. Lydia was more interested in a small display of powders and salves used to polish riding boots.

They had just concluded their purchase when the sound of the door opening and a distinctive voice hallooing attracted their attention.

The new patron was, in fact, Mrs Wardle-Penfield herself.

She was a woman with a definite presence. Her personality was so strong as to be almost palpable, and she did not merely enter a room but seemed rather to invade it and take its inhabitants captive at once.

Poor Aunt Camilla was quite overcome, stammering out her eternal gratitude for the unparalleled kindness and condescension of her would-be patroness in permitting the use of her carriage. Lydia, upon being introduced, added her own more quiet thanks.

'Nonsense!' Mrs Wardle-Penfield barked at them. 'What use have I for the carriage in this town? If I didn't need it to visit my brother in Hampshire now and again, I'd have sold it years ago. Not that my precious brother ever puts himself to the trouble of visiting *me*, mind you.'

'Oh, indeed—' Camilla began, apparently feeling the necessity for some comment. She need not have bothered, however, for the lady paid not the least heed to her.

'How many times,' she cried, her voice resounding through the shop as if she were singing an aria at Covent Garden, 'I have told my husband that the carriage is a ruinous waste of money, I do not know. After all, one can hire very fine vehicles at reasonable rates for the occasional jaunt. But the poor dear is so old-fashioned. He insists that our standards should not be lowered to that of cits and assorted mushrooms.'

'I think you are very wise, ma'am,' Lydia said sweetly, 'to draw attention to your superior station. If you did not, who would ever know of it?'

Mrs Wardle-Penfield frowned, not certain whether or not

she should construe this as a compliment. In the end she evidently decided that it could be nothing else, and continued with her soliloquy.

'I am sure, my dear Miss Denton,' she said with a pointed look, 'that you will want your niece to become acquainted with the most unexceptionable members of our little community. You shall both attend my card party on Friday next.'

This was not an invitation, but a command. The lady proceeded to enumerate the pleasures which awaited them at her residence. By the time she had passed from the quality of her refreshments to the weave of the carpet in her drawing room, Lydia was quite exhausted and Aunt Camilla no longer even bothered to nod her assent at every word, but merely stared stupidly at her tormentor, abandoning the struggle.

From this social purgatory they were rescued by the arrival of a large and rather awkward young gentleman, who seemed curiously impervious to the mesmerizing power of the older woman. This was a trait which endeared him to Lydia at once.

'Good morning, ma'am!' he called jovially to Mrs Wardle-Penfield. 'How d'ye do, Miss Denton?'

'You are very cheerful this fine morning, my lad!'

'Nothing to mope about, Mrs P,' he answered the old lady, who seemed none too pleased at being thus addressed.

'Have you been introduced to Miss Denton's niece?' Mrs Wardle-Penfield enquired.

'No,' he answered, 'but I don't mind if I do now.'

Aunt Camilla performed this necessary office, and Lydia received a hearty handshake from the gentleman, whose name was John Savidge. She judged him to be about her own age, with sandy hair cropped fashionably short and wide-open brown eyes. His suit was well-cut, though probably not by a London tailor. It was just a trifle too comfortable-looking for that.

'How does your grandmother get on?' Aunt Camilla asked him. 'She still lives in Piddinghoe, does she not?'

'Yes indeed, ma'am.' He gave a devilish grin. 'Not a day goes by that she doesn't threaten to cock up her toes, but I tell her she'll live to dance on all our graves.'

The young man's irreverent manner clearly did not suit Mrs Wardle-Penfield, who soon spied another victim passing outside the shop window and took herself off in pursuit of fresh sport.

Lydia and her aunt followed her outside, but mercifully their path led in the opposite direction. They were soon joined by Mr Savidge, who had concluded his own purchase and whose long strides easily bridged the short distance between them.

Almost as soon as he came up beside them, Lydia caught sight of a very distinctive physiognomy across the street from them.

'It's Nose!' The words came out before she could stop to consider.

'I beg your pardon?' Aunt Camilla turned to her with a look of wonder.

'Whose nose?' Mr Savidge asked, equally surprised, but apparently not so apprehensive of her sanity as her aunt

30

clearly was.

Despite herself, Lydia blushed.

'The gentleman across the street,' she confessed, being careful not to point or stare.

The other two directed their gaze to the opposite side of the high road. Nose was engaged in a conversation with another man who was certainly much better-looking and quite a few years younger.

'It is Monsieur d'Almain!' Her aunt seemed suddenly rather breathless, the colour rising to her cheeks.

'I think, ma'am,' Mr Savidge said with a smile, 'that she is referring to the other gentleman.'

'Oh.'

'He was in the seat opposite me on the Mail,' Lydia informed them hastily. 'I – well, I could not forget his face.'

'I should think not, indeed!' John Savidge agreed. 'With that great big thing stuck in the middle of it.'

Lydia found it difficult to suppress a fit of giggles at his words, which so exactly corresponded with her own impression. However, while she struggled to retain command of herself, Nose bowed to the other gentleman – Monsieur d'Almain, it would seem – and proceeded along the pavement. At that moment, d'Almain became aware of their presence, doffed his own hat and bowed toward them. He did not attempt to join them, but turned and walked away.

'Not a bad fellow, for a Frenchman,' Mr Savidge commented. 'Keeps to himself most of the time, but a real gentleman.'

'Indeed he is,' Aunt Camilla said, with what Lydia deemed a degree of fervor quite disproportionate to the subject.

'Well, I must be off,' John said gaily. 'Good day, ladies.'

So saying, he entered the inn by which they were passing.

'Who is he?' Lydia asked when he had left them.

'John?' Aunt Camilla asked, somewhat distracted.

'Yes.'

'His father owns the inn,' her aunt explained.

'He seems very pleasant.'

'Most good-natured,' she agreed, glancing behind them and to the left, where the two gentlemen had so recently been standing. 'Quite wealthy too. It's a pity that his family's fortune is acquired from trade.'

'What fustian!' Lydia dismissed this social blemish in two disdainful words.

'Perhaps.'

Lydia eyed her aunt curiously. She was hardly attending to what was being said, lost in a strange reverie. It was not difficult to connect this with the appearance of Monsieur d'Almain.

Smiling to herself, Lydia considered that her morning had been far more eventful than she had anticipated. She had received an invitation to a card party (even though it was issued by an old harridan), been introduced to an attractive young gentleman, and discovered what appeared to be a budding romance between her aunt and a mysterious Frenchman. It could not be more promising!

The countryside was plainly more entertaining than most people guessed. Her visit might be many things, but it would not be dull.

CHAPTER FOUR

BLOODY MURDER

It was the unanimous opinion of all who attended Mrs Wardle-Penfield's card party that the occasion was a resounding success. Not that Mrs Wardle-Penfield would have tolerated anything else, but this time she did not need to bully anyone into expressing unqualified approval.

It was not the indifferent skills of the various players which produced such a favourable verdict. Neither whist nor speculation could animate the guests who had antici-pated having to endure what could not be cured. The stakes were low, though not so low as the expectations of the select company which gathered in the large drawing-room of Fielding Place on that memorable evening.

What ensured that nobody departed dissatisfied with their lot was a rumour so incredible and so horrifying that several games were suspended altogether in the recounting of its manifold details. These became so elaborate and were related with such conviction that it was not very long before the truth was lost beneath an avalanche of fancy. For this was no ordinary *on-dit* involving pilfering by a servant nor the latest escapades of the Carlton House set. Neither was it the far-off rumblings of fear that Bonaparte might have escaped from St Helena to once again wreak havoc on the Continent. This was closer to home – indeed, on their very doorstep. And this was no light matter. It was murder.

Lydia and Aunt Camilla had no inkling of what awaited them as they prepared for the party. Lydia derived some amusement from her aunt, whose nerves were quite overset at the thought that she might commit some dreadful *faux pas* in the presence of her illustrious hostess. She tweaked every curl in her simple coiffure, smoothed every wrinkle in her wheat-coloured satin gown at least a dozen times, and murmured dire prognostications about the weather. It seemed a grim inevitability that the heavens must open at the very moment that they were making their way on foot to their appointed destination. The deluge would cover them with mud from head to foot, making them the laughing stock of the other guests.

No such terrors dampened the spirits of her niece. Lydia surveyed herself practically in the mirror above the small mantel in the parlour. Her hair curled naturally, so she had little recourse to hot irons. Aside from this boon, there was little remarkable about her appearance. The creamy muslin of her gown made her skin appear rather sallow, and her gloves were a trifle worn, but she was satisfied that most would not notice these defects and, if they did, there was nothing to be done about it in any case. One must be philosophical, after all. It was not as if she were a beauty.

She expected no heads to turn upon her entrance, unless she tripped over her train.

As usual, she was correct in her assumption. Entering the abode of which she had heard so much these past three days, they were greeted with gracious condescension by Mrs Wardle-Penfield, and hustled off to a whist table where they were introduced to their partners, the Misses Digweed. These were two middle-aged spinster sisters who resided not far from their own house. It was from the lips of these two garrulous ladies that Lydia and her aunt first heard the news.

They had been involved in play for several minutes, and Lydia was already learning that her aunt was not the ideal partner. Lydia was an accomplished player who regularly bested Papa, but Camilla seemed doubtful as to what game they were playing. She frequently forgot to follow suit, and it soon became clear that they were almost certainly destined to lose. There was nothing Lydia could do, but sigh softly to herself and accept her fate as gracefully as possible.

'I suppose,' the younger Miss Digweed said, with an arch look at Aunt Camilla over the top of her cards, 'that you have heard about the murder, Miss Denton?'

'Murder!'

Lydia feared that her aunt was going to swoon. She clutched her cards against her breast while something resembling a spasm passed across her face.

'Oh dear!' the other Miss Digweed cried. 'It seems that you have *not* heard.'

It was an opportunity too enticing to resist. There is

nothing so sweet as the pleasure of being the very first to relate bad news to a listener who hangs upon every word. In this case, they were doubly fortunate in having not one but two auditors who received their story with all the wide-eyed attention they could have desired.

The tale unfolded so rapidly, and with such fluctuations from one Miss Digweed to the other, that Lydia was soon uncertain as to just what had happened – and indeed, whether anything had happened at all.

'A young woman—' Miss Janet Digweed began.

'No, no,' Miss Digweed corrected her at once. 'An old man.'

'In Wickham Wood.'

'Or very near it.'

'Stabbed—'

'Beaten—'

'Found yesterday morning—'

'Evening—'

'By young Tom Fowle—'

'His brother, Jimmy—'

'Dreadful!'

'Horrible!'

'But – but is it certain?' Aunt Camilla at last halted this interesting narrative. 'I cannot believe it!'

'Forgive me,' Lydia cut in, addressing both sisters at once. 'Who has been killed?'

The Misses Digweed appeared quite startled. Such a question had apparently never occurred to either of them.

'Well really,' the elder answered, 'we do not know.'

'Nobody knows.'

'But someone is certainly dead.'

'It reminds me of the other time,' Aunt Camilla said, her lips trembling pitifully. 'I never thought—'

'I think,' Lydia said decisively, 'that you had best have a seat on the sofa, Aunt. You have had a shock.'

The sisters smiled kindly upon their neighbour, pleased with their share in her discomfort.

'Perhaps some negus,' Miss Digweed offered helpfully.

'A glass of wine,' her sister suggested.

Excusing herself happily from their company, Lydia led her aunt to a corner of the room which was then unoccupied. Signalling to a servant, she managed to procure a small glass of brandy, which she forced upon her aunt. All this attracted the attention of their hostess, who bore down upon them purposefully.

'What is the matter?' she demanded, looming over the two seated on the sofa.

'Dear Mrs Wardle-Penfield,' Aunt Camilla whispered, 'I had not heard until tonight. I did not know. . . .'

'What are you saying, Camilla?' the older woman asked, with justifiable irritation.

'We have just been told about the death in Wickham Wood,' Lydia answered for her.

'Oh, that.' The murder was dismissed with a slight shrug and a twist of the lips which conveyed the impression that murder was a social solecism of which Mrs Wardle-Penfield definitely did not approve. 'Some drunken lout, I'll warrant, who fell and dashed his head against a stone.'

'Does anyone know the identity of the dead . . . man?' Lydia enquired hesitantly.

'I should think not!' the haughty dame was scandalized at the suggestion. 'Such persons assuredly do not move in our circles.'

Having thus distanced herself from anyone who was so ill-bred as to permit himself to be murdered, she returned to the subject of her dear friend's nerves. Declaring that Aunt Camilla's constitution was far too delicate, and that it was a wonder she was so well-preserved for her age, she recommended Doctor Humbleby's Tonic as an unfailing remedy for anyone prone to the vapours. Then, with a bracing pat on the shoulder, she returned to her other guests.

Miss Denton's distress, however, had been perceived by at least one interested onlooker. The French gentleman, Monsieur d'Almain soon made his way over to them. He expressed genuine concern, and his gentleness and soothing murmurs soon had a calming affect upon the afflicted lady.

Perhaps a quarter of an hour passed before her aunt had recovered sufficiently to rejoin the whist players. The company had increased considerably by that time, and there did not appear to be many openings for another partner at any of the tables. Eventually, a place was found for Camilla. However, Lydia was left to her seat against the wall. This was very much to her liking, as she did not relish sharing a table with her aunt. It was much more interesting to sit quietly and observe the assembled company. It was better for her aunt to be occupied, in any case, so that she did not have an opportunity to dwell upon the tragedy.

Within a very few minutes, Lydia spied a large head protruding above the others in the room. It was the young gentlemen they had met a few days before: Mr Savidge. Despite his boyish looks, she had learned that he was on the brink of achieving his majority. To her surprise, he soon made his way over to her and established himself on the settee beside her.

'You are not playing, Mr Savidge?' she asked him, once the obligatory greetings had been dispensed with.

'Don't like cards,' he confessed. 'Waste of time, if you ask me. Prefer the races myself.'

'Do you often visit Lewes?'

'As often as I'm able.'

'I know little about horseflesh,' Lydia said apologetically. 'But I must confess that it does sound more entertaining than such an evening as this.'

'It could hardly be less entertaining, could it?'

His face folded into a mischievous smile which was quite infectious.

'You find life in Diddlington a dead bore?' she asked him boldly.

'Oh, it's not so terrible.' He shrugged philosophically. 'I mean, one makes the most of whatever's offered.'

'The Misses Digweed have informed us that there has been a rather . . . unusual death in the vicinity of the woods hereabouts.'

'Indeed.' He nodded. 'I make no doubt they made a pretty mess of it.'

Lydia giggled. 'I can hardly be sure whether the corpse is male or female.'

40

'To tell you the truth,' he lowered his voice, leaning his head toward her somewhat conspiratorially, 'it was hard for anyone to tell much about it. Very nasty, I assure you.'

'You have actually seen the body?' She could not quite disguise the envy in her voice. Gentlemen always seemed to have more fun than ladies.

'Oh yes,' he said, not boasting but simply as a matter of course. 'My father is Diddlington's Justice of the Peace.'

'Is he?' She was surprised. 'I had thought your father owned the Golden Cockerel.'

'So he does,' young Mr Savidge said. 'But he's also one of the wealthiest men in town. By rights, Sir Hector Mannington should be the JP, but he's over ninety and not up to snuff any longer, poor man.'

'And you say that the person who was murdered was unrecognizable.'

'Seems to me,' John Savidge said with slow deliberation, 'that somebody wanted to make certain that he wasn't recognized.'

'How so?'

'Well, the face had been smashed in with a large stone which was found nearby. Also—'

Here, their little tête-à-tête was interrupted by Mr Savidge's father himself. Like his son, Mr Thomas Savidge was a large, beefy-handed man. But whereas the younger man seemed to have a rather placid disposition, the innkeeper was a loud, boisterous fellow whose voice could have substituted for a hunting horn. He immediately took over the conversation, paying outrageous compliments to Lydia which she took no heed of since it was clear that they were simply what Mr Savidge mistakenly believed to be proper etiquette in addressing young ladies.

'You mustn't prose on about horses or anything to this fair damsel, John,' he chafed his son. 'Don't want her to be bored by idle chatter.'

'We were discussing the murder,' Lydia informed him.

Mr Savidge frowned. 'What a cod's head you are, boy!' he cried loudly, causing several heads to turn in his direction. 'A fine thing to be filling a young lady's head with nightmares and such. You have no notion how to get on, my boy! Flirting: that's the ticket.'

'Oh, I do not mind at all,' Lydia hastened to inform him. 'I find it absolutely fascinating. And I assure you, I know no more of flirtation than your son does.'

The innkeeper would have none of it, however. He continued to instruct his son in quite improper ways of dealing with the fair sex, until he was finally abducted by Mrs Wardle-Penfield and incarcerated at one of the card tables. Lydia and John were therefore free to resume their discussion.

'Sorry about m'father,' John muttered.

'Oh, don't be!' Lydia said. 'I thought him prodigiously amusing.'

'He can be a little – overwhelming.'

'I am surprised that his hostess can so easily control him,' she answered with more truth than tact.

'No trouble in that quarter.' John chuckled. 'Papa thinks Mrs P can do no wrong. Hopes to rise in society under her patronage.'

'And you?'

'Oh, I've no such ambitions.'

'Thank goodness for that!' Lydia was very pleased by her companion's easy, unaffected manners. He neither was, nor considered himself to be of the gentry. It was most refreshing.

'No use pretending to be what you ain't. I may have been educated at Harrow, but I'm an innkeeper's son and not ashamed of it.'

'But tell me more about the murder,' she persisted.

'Whoever the guilty party might be,' John told her, 'they either had a grudge against the victim or didn't mean for anyone to know his identity.'

'But the victim *is* a man?'

'Definitely.'

'Horribly disfigured by a stone, though. . . .'

'More than that, Miss Bramwell.'

'Good heavens! What more could there be?'

'The body was covered in oil and lit on fire—'

Lydia caught her breath. It was better than she could ever have imagined.

'How horrible!' she breathed. 'No wonder that nobody can tell who it is.'

'I have my suspicions.'

'Do you?' She eyed him with growing respect.

'I'm almost certain it's your friend, the Nose.'

In spite of herself Lydia blushed. Still, she could not allow embarrassment to spoil her fun.

'The gentleman from the Mail?'

'That's right. A Mr Cole.' John nodded emphatically. 'He was putting up at the inn, but hasn't been seen in several days. Left his bag and his belongings there, though.'

'Could it really be him?'

'I'd bet a goodly sum on it.'

Lydia glanced around the room at the smiling, gesticulating group. Her eye fell on an ornate clock which graced the mantel on the opposite side of the room and a sudden thought came to her.

'Do you know if there was a silver watch found on the – the body?' she asked.

A look of surprise crossed the face of Mr Savidge. 'I believe there was.'

'Carved with some kind of grotesque faces?'

'The masks of Comedy and Tragedy.'

'I saw him take it out several times on the journey,' she explained. 'I believe he wanted to impress Ears with it.'

Naturally, she then had to explain the curious appendages of Mr Cole's travelling companion, which almost caused John to go into whoops. When he had gained control of himself, he said that he would pass along this information to his father. It seemed that the dead man had now been identified beyond all reasonable doubt.

CHAPTER FIVE

A NEW FRIEND

'But then,' Lydia said to her aunt the next morning as they sat together over their breakfast, 'it makes no sense.'

'I do wish you would leave off this subject, Lydia,' Aunt Camilla protested faintly. 'My nerves are all a-jangle as it is.'

Of course there was no possibility of ignoring such a momentous event, even had Lydia wished to do so. However, she had no such wish.

'If the motive for killing Mr Cole was robbery,' she persisted, heedless of her aunt's sensibilities, 'why was his watch not taken? From the looks of it, I'd wager it was his most valuable possession.'

'Well then, there must have been another motive,' her aunt snapped, apparently accepting the fact that there was no escaping her niece's morbid fascination with this unfortunate incident.

'Precisely. But what reason could there possibly be?'

Lydia demanded. 'Why would anyone in Diddlington murder a perfect stranger?'

'Perhaps it was an accident,' Camilla suggested hopefully.

'I think it unlikely that anyone could accidentally smash someone's head in with a stone; nor could they set fire to the corpse in error.'

Camilla shuddered at the vivid images which this speech conjured up in her mind.

'Please . . .' she whispered, fortifying her nerves with a few sips of strong Gunpowder Tea.

'John thinks that it was all an attempt to disguise the identity of the victim. But then it would be foolish to leave the watch. Of course,' she mused aloud, 'that may have been an oversight.'

'I daresay one can be quite forgetful when committing a murder.'

This was a more trenchant remark than was usual for her soft-spoken relation, so Lydia deemed it politic to keep any further conjectures to herself. If she wished to discuss the matter with anyone, the most logical person was John Savidge. He was in a position to know more than any other of her aunt's acquaintance, and he certainly seemed more intelligent than anyone else she had met in Diddlington.

Her estimation of the mental powers of the village's inhabitants was not improved by developments over the following week. No sooner had the first wave of astonishment crashed upon the imaginations of the populace than it was followed by a surging tide of superstition and fantastic supposition.

From the meanest yeoman farmer to the most exalted residents of the hamlet, speculation swelled from a furtive whisper to the deafening roar of a mighty torrent.

To begin with, there was what was now grandly termed the 'previous incident'. This telling phrase referred to another murder which had occurred some three years before in almost the same spot. Nobody had ever been charged, and the unsolved crime had been banished from the collective imagination of Diddlingtonians until it was brought so forcefully to mind by what appeared to be its twin.

'Horrible it was!' Mr Berwick, the vicar, intoned piously, when Aunt Camilla mentioned the matter to him. He had called to see how the two ladies got on and, naturally, he did not refuse the offer of tea – especially since he had timed his visit precisely at the hour when he knew it would be offered to him.

'Dear Mr Berwick,' Camilla said, catching her lips between her teeth to keep them from trembling. 'What has anyone in Diddlington done to deserve this – this display of divine wrath?'

'The wrath in this case seems rather human than divine,' Lydia opined before the gentleman could respond.

'Indeed, you are quite right Miss Bramwell,' the good man agreed. 'The human heart, as the Scripture saith, "is deceitful above all things and desperately evil." Who can know the evil hidden within it?'

This did little to console the elder of his two charming companions. Camilla continued to bemoan such a terrible occurrence until Mr Berwick's stomach was full and he dismissed himself.

But while he might be of the same mind as Lydia, others had far more dramatic views of what had happened in the darkness of Wickham Wood. It was said that the wood had once been the meeting place of a coven of witches. Many expressed the view that the spirits of these long-dead practitioners of the Black Arts continued to haunt the groves where their perverse ceremonies had been held.

'The Devil is in it, mark my words!' This phrase, or some variation thereof, was heard more than once on the street and in the tavern where the men gathered to while away the evening hours.

But even this was not enough to satisfy those who apparently had read *The Monk* one too many times. Knowing that Mr Cole's corpse had been burned beyond recognition, these folks looked back toward an even more distant and mysterious past. There were local legends of a fire-breathing dragon which had menaced the countryside in the days of St Augustine. The hardy old saint had vanquished him with a silver crucifix. Perhaps this beast had risen, phoenix-like, from the ashes and was bent on reclaiming what was left of the woodlands he had once inhabited!

Lydia hardly knew whether to laugh or weep when she heard one of the maids solemnly express this charming theory to another servant – who seemed much impressed and easily persuaded. For herself, she rather suspected a more alarming beast which walked on two legs and used two hands to accomplish what serpentine scales and monstrous wings could not.

Mrs Wardle-Penfield refused to entertain the possibility that anyone in their village could have committed such an atrocity. However, her theories on the subject came perilously close to creating a rift between her and Aunt Camilla.

'Not one of *our* people could have been involved,' she declared.

'What do you mean, ma'am?' Aunt Camilla stiffened slightly.

'It must have been someone from outside the village,' the older woman explained, as though to a child.

'Of whom are you thinking?'

'Frankly,' Mrs Wardle-Penfield stated, 'I would look into that Frenchman, if I were Mr Savidge.'

'That is absurd – and slanderous!'

Lydia had hardly believed that her aunt could be so animated. She fairly trembled in her outrage.

'I know that you have a partiality for him, my dear Camilla, though it seems absurd at your age,' her friend replied, not a whit perturbed. 'But what do we really know about the man?'

'We know that he was not living here when the other murder occurred,' Camilla flung at her, as if to say, 'There! Explain that, if you can.' Mrs Wardle-Penfield did.

'Monsieur d'Almain arrived to take up residence in Diddlington very soon after that incident,' she reminded her with a speaking glance. 'Who knows where he might have been hiding before that?'

'Hiding!'

'Of course,' the *grande dame* added graciously, 'he may

not have been involved in that case. But that is no reason to suppose him innocent in this.'

'Is there any reason to suspect him, ma'am,' Lydia asked drily, 'other than the fact that he is French?'

'Is that not enough?' She seemed surprised. 'After all, one cannot trust the French. Look at Bonaparte!'

'I believe,' Lydia returned, 'that Napoleon is from Corsica, not France.'

The lady shrugged. 'It is all one.'

'I recall that Monsieur d'Almain was a guest at your own card party only recently.'

'My dear Camilla,' the lady protested, growing slightly defensive, 'you know as well as I do that he has the *entrée* everywhere. There is a sad dearth of eligible gentlemen in this parish, and one must make do with what one has.'

'I do hope,' Aunt Camilla said, barely squeezing the words through clenched teeth, 'that you have not mentioned your suspicions to anyone.'

Mrs Wardle-Penfield adjusted the lace collar on her elaborate morning-gown before responding, 'I did drop a word in Mr Savidge's ear. However, I doubt that he paid any heed to it. Not the smartest hound in the pack, Mr Savidge. I would never expect him to corner the fox, myself.'

'I'm sure,' the other lady raised her chin again, 'he is far too sensible to be suspecting Monsieur d'Almain of something so vile.'

'Young John,' her friend continued, deaf to her outburst, 'is another matter.'

'Is he?' Lydia enquired, a little surprised to find herself in agreement with the lady.

'He may play the schoolboy,' Mrs Wardle-Penfield informed them, 'but Master John is as sharp as they come, in spite of his impertinent manner.'

This last remark no doubt referred to his lack of deference toward herself, Lydia thought with an inward chuckle which she barely managed to contain.

CHAPTER SIX

A DARING PLAN

Lydia was able to draw Aunt Camilla away from her friend
before an irrevocable schism could develop between them.
It was some time before her aunt could at all regain her
composure. No sooner had she done so, in fact, than she lost
it again. Her mind was only now able to comprehend Mrs
Wardle-Penfield's remark concerning her partiality for the
Frenchman.

'Oh!' she exclaimed, her cheeks reddening. 'I hope that
she does not imagine that I am setting my cap at Monsieur
d'Almain.'

'No,' Lydia offered by way of cold comfort. 'She merely
perceives what everyone must: that you have a decided
tendre for the man.'

'It is not true!' Camilla cried, rising precipitately from her
chair and wringing her hands. 'I do indeed admire him—'

'Indeed.'

'But do you suppose that he suspects – that he believes—'

'Calm yourself, dear aunt.' Lydia rose also, gently pressing her aunt back onto her chair. 'Nobody could ever accuse you of flirting, you know. It is not in your nature. I am sure that your behaviour toward Monsieur d'Almain has always been well within the bounds of propriety.'

'Yes,' her aunt whispered somewhat mournfully.

'In fact,' Lydia went on with her usual forthright but tactless commonsense, 'you will never attach him if you do not make more of a push.'

'Lydia!' For a moment it seemed Camilla would swoon at this vulgar sentiment. 'You really should not say such things.'

'Well, I would not do so to a stranger.' She looked down upon her aunt with mild disapprobation. 'But we are family, and need not be coy about such things. It is foolish to pretend that you would not welcome a proposal from the man.'

'I am sure he never thought of such a thing,' Camilla said primly.

'And never will, if you do not encourage him.'

'I – I do not know how to do so.'

'No.' Lydia sighed. 'If you did know, you probably would have married long before now.'

'There are worse things than being an old maid.'

'Not if you desire something more,' her niece answered tartly.

A tremulous smile touched her aunt's pink lips. 'You are right, of course.'

'Well, we must contrive between us.'

She perceived a look of alarm in her aunt's eyes. Camilla

Denton was a woman of strong feelings but not equally strong will. She would sit and dream her life away in single-blessedness unless something was done about it.

'What are you planning, Lydia?' Camilla asked.

'I must give the matter more consideration.' Lydia looked thoughtfully through the parlour window and happened to see John Savidge walking past the house. 'Excuse me, dear aunt!' she cried, vaulting up. 'I will be back directly.'

If John was put out by being accosted on his way to the inn, he displayed no sign of it. When Lydia hailed him, he turned and smiled warmly at her before retracing his steps to the gate of her aunt's cottage.

'Miss Bramwell.' He doffed his hat. 'How d'ye do?'

'Quite well, Mr Savidge,' she replied politely. 'Can you spare a few minutes, sir?'

'Of course I can.'

She ushered him into her aunt's parlour, where Camilla sat looking somewhat discomfited. She so rarely entertained any gentlemen callers beyond the vicar and the occasional tradesman. Still, John was well known to her and she would soon have composed herself had not her niece immediately broached a subject which never failed to overset her nerves.

'Have you discovered any more about the murder?' Lydia demanded.

'Lydia!' Camilla begged, her hand clutching her throat as though to keep the breath from escaping entirely.

'There seems to be nothing more to discover,' John answered.

'I suppose you have heard the rumours circulating in the village?'

'Dragons and demons?' He shook his head, half amused and half disgusted. 'Superstitions die hard in the country.'

Lydia leaned forward, determined to know more. He clearly thought as little of the prevailing notions as did she.

'What is your opinion of the matter?' she asked pointedly.

'Do not be plaguing John about this,' her aunt pleaded, referring to Mr Savidge with the casual air of one who had known him from his cradle.

'But I cannot get it out of my mind,' Lydia protested to both of them, refusing to be put off. 'I am convinced that there is more to this than meets the eye.'

'I quite agree, Miss Bramwell.'

John's response both surprised and delighted her. At last here was someone who did not settle for easy answers. He was as concerned as she was that someone – who for now must be unknown – should profit by a crime so heinous.

'I can bear no more of this!' Aunt Camilla cried, and made haste to quit the room, leaving the two young people alone together in a most improper manner which neither of them considered for a moment.

'Should you not go to her?' John asked, frowning at the retreating form of his hostess.

'Oh no!' Lydia dismissed the suggestion carelessly. 'Best to let her enjoy her vapours in private. She will feel much more the thing afterward, I assure you.'

He accepted this without demur, and they returned to the topic which most interested them both. After all, in such restricted society there was not much to exercise the mental faculties and stir the imagination of young people. Mr Cole's death was a source of endless entertainment, and they would have scarcely been human had they not found something in it to occupy their minds. It was merely that they both looked more deeply into the matter than the generality of their neighbours.

'My father,' John said at length, 'is inclined to blame the matter on gypsies. That solution would certainly be the simplest one.'

'Do you think it likely?'

'Well, no gypsies or mendicants have been seen in the area for some time, to my knowledge.'

'And it seems that you have discounted—' she coughed delicately, 'any supernatural agency.'

'I have.'

'Then where do your suspicions lie?'

He stroked his chin pensively before continuing.

'I think it very likely that smugglers, rather than phantoms, are involved.'

'Smugglers!' Lydia's cry was one of scandalized delight. It was better and better.

'You seem surprised,' John said with a smile.

'I am.'

John immediately set about the task of educating her concerning the history of Sussex. It seemed that smuggling had at one time been a very lucrative source of income for certain persons along the southeast coast of England. Even since the defeat of Napoleon, the Alfriston Gang and others were known to have continued this less than respectable profession. Some had been caught and prosecuted by the Crown, providing the gibbet with a few gruesome trophies.

'You think,' Lydia said, 'that there may be a Diddlington Gang, and that Mr Cole had some connection with them?'

'It is possible.' John was a little more cautious in his assessment.

'How can we prove it?' she asked.

'We?' His smile now was very pronounced, as was the arch of one thick eyebrow.

'You and I,' she explained with casual assurance.

'If we could discover where they conceal their stolen goods,' he said, not contradicting her, 'we would certainly go some way toward solving this riddle.'

'Do you think it is in Wickham Wood?'

'I am almost certain.' He nodded emphatically. 'Too many local folk have seen lights among the trees at night and even a few sober men claim to have encountered ghostly apparitions in the vicinity.'

'An excellent means for the smugglers to frighten away anyone who might venture too near their hiding place.'

'Precisely.'

Lydia stood up, looking down at him in a glow of excited anticipation.

'Then there is only one thing to be done!' she cried. 'We must go into the woods ourselves and find the smugglers' lair.'

'I think,' John said dampingly, 'that is a job which I should attempt on my own.'

This was totally unacceptable to Lydia.

'If you think that you can keep me out of this adventure,

John Savidge,' she told him roundly, 'you are much mistaken.'

'Your aunt would never permit it,' he shot back reasonably.

'Which is why,' Lydia retorted with a smile, 'I have no intention of telling her anything about it.'

'Minx!' he quizzed her. 'And what will become of her when someone discovers *our* bodies at the edge of the wood?'

For a moment she paused, considering this not improbable consequence of confronting a gang of dangerous malefactors. However, although it was totally irrational, she felt complete confidence in John's ability to extricate them from any difficulty which might result from their rash behaviour.

'Are you afraid?' she demanded, quizzing him in her turn.

'Oh no!' He grinned broadly at her. 'I know that I have nothing to fear with *you* there to protect me.'

And so the two became co-conspirators in a daring plan whose effects would prove more momentous than either of them could possibly imagine.

CHAPTER SEVEN

A SAD DISAPPOINTMENT

Midnight. The moon was full and round as a silver tray resting on the ebony table of the sky. Lydia had considered climbing through the window of her bedroom. She abandoned this scheme not only because of its impracticality, but because it was simply unnecessary. Her aunt and old Mrs Plumpton were both fast asleep by the time the two hands on the clock pointed heavenward, so Lydia slipped from her room and wandered the house at will, leaving it through the side door of the kitchen.

She flattered herself that she would not be recognized, even if anyone happened to be about at this hour. As Providence would have it, Aunt Camilla had taken in some clothes to darn before distributing them amongst the poor of the parish. Out of this miscellany, Lydia had purloined a pair of rough pantaloons, a shirt and a short coat. In this attire, she looked more like an urchin than a young lady of seventeen.

Striding down the lane in the moonlight, the only one who noticed her was the neighbour's cat, Cecilia. This curious feline followed at her heels for awhile, before a movement in the underbrush attracted her attention and she disappeared in search of a hapless mouse.

Within ten minutes, Lydia reached the edge of the town. She leaned against an oak tree and waited. The stillness was almost palpable, and more forbidding than she had anticipated. It was with relief that she heard the thud-thud of hooves and observed John leading his horse, Scapegrace, toward her.

'Well met, my lad!' John greeted her in a loud whisper when he drew near enough.

This reference to her male costume did not discompose her. She merely replied, 'I thought skirts would be very much in the way.'

'I do not disagree with you.' He helped her up onto Scapegrace before mounting behind her. 'But for a moment I thought you had sent someone else in your place.'

'And miss this adventure?' He must be mad. 'There is small chance of that!'

They rode slowly at first, and then at a pretty brisk gallop. Lydia was not really accustomed to being on horse-back, but she found it quite exhilarating; nor was she in the least afraid, with John's arms about her and his broad chest for support.

'What is that house there?' she asked, seeing a silver silhouette rising above a neat expanse of parkland.

'That's Bellefleur, Sir Hector Mannington's place.'

'I've heard my aunt speak of him.' Lydia looked more

intently, though not in expectation of seeing anything. 'He is something of a recluse, is he not?'

'And old as Methuselah,' John added.

'They say that he is mad as a hatter, and treats his servants shamefully.'

'They also say that there are ghosts haunting Wickham Wood,' he reminded her.

She acknowledged the good sense of this remark, refraining from further comments. A few minutes later, John reined in his horse and dismounted. He reached up and helped Lydia down as well.

'From here, we walk.'

'Is it far?' she asked, watching him tether Scapegrace to a sturdy tree trunk.

'Less than a mile.'

'But why stop here?'

'Because,' he answered, turning back to her, 'something as large as a horse is difficult to hide. If there *are* smugglers in the wood, we don't want to announce our presence, do we?'

'No indeed.'

For the next fifteen minutes, they walked silently together through the fields in the moonlight. Scrambling over stiles and navigating ha-has, they gradually made their way toward a patch of impenetrable darkness outlined against the sky. At length John broke the silence with a loud whisper.

'This is where Mr Cole was found.'

Lydia almost jumped out of her pantaloons as she looked down on a patch of ground which showed evidence of a recent fire. To think that some of those ashes beneath her feet might actually be the remains of a dead man! Even the smell of the place was unpleasant: the scent of desecration, perhaps? It was an eerie feeling indeed, and she was conscious of a desire to quit the spot as soon as possible.

'Poor man!' she declared sententiously. 'I hope that he did not suffer too much.'

'My father said there was hardly a patch of skin remaining on the bones.' John's statement was dispassionate, as if he were describing a portrait hanging in an old house. 'The few bits of flesh left were so seared by the flames that they looked like the skin of a centenarian.'

'How awful!' Lydia breathed excitedly. 'And to think it was the second corpse to be discovered in such a fashion.'

'Not precisely,' John said after a brief pause.

'What do you mean?'

'The previous corpse was not burnt,' he explained.

Lydia was startled, though she was not sure why she should be.

'I had thought the deaths were identical,' she said, half to herself.

'Why?'

'Well, it seems to me that a murderer who takes the time to kill two people in the same place is more than likely to employ the same method. Of course,' she continued with some self-deprecation, 'I am not well versed in such matters.'

'No,' John agreed. 'Not but what I think you have the right of it. I never considered the matter before.'

'Perhaps the two crimes are quite unrelated.'

'Just what I was thinking.'

'But that is almost more difficult to believe.' Lydia shook her head. 'There must be a connection, only we have not yet perceived it.'

'Come,' John said, linking his arm with hers. 'Hold on to me. We must not become separated.'

He had scarcely finished speaking before he drew her after him into the woods. The change was so immediate and so dramatic that Lydia actually gave a gasp of surprise. The moonlight beyond the wood was crisply bright, making their progress quite easy. However, once beneath the canopy of the trees, a curtain of gloomy darkness descended upon them.

There were shapes and shadows all around, to be sure, but they were mysterious and unrecognizable. It was a cool evening, but it was not the chill air which made Lydia tremble suddenly and tighten her hold upon John's arm.

A loud rustling and the sound of something swooping down out of the trees almost deprived her of speech. Could the villagers be right? Did these woods harbour demonic spirits? Lydia watched the shadowy creature wing its way amongst the oak and birch trees, her heart pounding uncomfortably in her breast.

'An owl,' John said shortly.

'Of course.' Lydia was pleased to note that she sounded far more composed than she felt.

Other denizens of the woods contributed to a subdued

symphony of night sounds as they made their way gingerly to the edge of a small circular clearing where the moonlight drifted down to settle in alabaster puddles upon the nodding leaves of enchanter's nightshade and the rounded heads of death-cap mushrooms. John pointed out – and carefully avoided – a sett of badgers. Meanwhile, a stoat poked its head out from a hawthorn bush before making a noisy exit into the darkness.

Lydia could understand now how the villagers might suppose supernatural agents to be at work here. Had her imagination been inclined in that direction, she could easily have convinced herself of the same thing. But despite what might justly be referred to as the relentless *ominosity* of the above description, she remained in command of her emotions and behaved with admirable presence of mind.

'We'd best sit down here and wait,' John said at last, pausing beside the trunk of a large oak tree.

He pulled off his jacket and laid it on the ground, motioning for her to make use of it as a makeshift cushion.

'Why this spot?' she enquired, looking around her and seeing nothing.

'It's as reasonable as any other part of the wood,' he replied, joining her on the ground. 'We are not in the centre, but we are deep enough to hear any unusual sound and to have some notion of where it comes from.'

'But what if the smugglers come from the other side?'

'Then we will doubtless miss them.'

Lydia was not certain that she approved of this phlegmatic attitude. Secretly, she considered that John should be a little more concerned that they might lose their quarry. It was an odd sort of hunter who cared not whether he caught his prey! However, she could scarcely argue the point, since he had been kind enough to include her in this adventure – which he was under no obligation to do, after all.

She gradually grew accustomed to the peculiar night sounds around them, and soon ceased to look up at every rustle in the underbrush. Conversation was kept to the barest minimum, as their situation dictated silence.

Eventually, boredom overcame the feeling of excited anticipation with which the night began. Without being aware of it, Lydia's head began to tilt ever so slightly. At some point in the proceedings, she fell asleep. It was only when the sound of her name roused her that she raised her head from John's shoulder, where it had been resting in surprising comfort.

'What?' she cried, looking about her in some confusion at first, until she remembered where they were and for what purpose. 'Did you hear something, John?'

'No,' John answered flatly. 'But it will be daylight in little more than an hour. We must go.'

'Are you certain that nothing happened?' she demanded.

'I assure you,' he said, with a grin, 'I would not have allowed you to sleep through an encounter with a gang of ruffians!'

With that, Lydia had to be content.

Their retreat from the woods was not nearly as interesting as their journey of a few hours before. It was an ignominious end to what had seemed a grand adventure. So much for romantic dreams. Lydia chided herself for having expected more. She was as hopeless as Louisa.

However, John remained undaunted.

'It is hardly likely,' he said as they rode back toward town in the darkness, 'that these fellows would frequent the wood every night. We must try again another night – perhaps when the moon is not full.'

'Do you think it likely that we will have better luck a second time?'

'Bound to!' he said cheerfully.

As Lydia made her way up to her bedchamber shortly thereafter, she was not so hopeful. Nor did she relish the thought of spending another night in the dark, inhospitable surroundings of Wickham Wood. Her enthusiasm was seriously dampened, along with her vitality. She was weary to her bones, and fell into bed at once.

It was quite late when she arose the next morning, and Aunt Camilla was all concern at the dark circles beneath her niece's eyes.

'Perhaps you are ill,' she suggested apprehensively, placing a hand on Lydia's brow to assure herself that there was no fever. 'I hope that it is not the influenza.'

'Has anyone in the village contracted influenza?' Lydia asked reasonably.

'No.' Her aunt paused, before adding, 'But it has to start with someone, does it not?'

'I am perfectly well, aunt,' Lydia said. 'I did not sleep very soundly last night. That is all.'

'Is something troubling you?' Camilla was still convinced

that ill health was the root of the problem. 'It is this terrible murder! Indeed, I do not know how anyone can sleep.'

'Yes, Aunt.' Lydia was glad to be able to answer with at least some semblance of truth. 'I fear that is my problem.'

They had scarcely swallowed the last morsel of breakfast, when a diversion was created by the arrival of a letter. It was addressed to Lydia, and was from London.

'It's from Papa!' Lydia exclaimed, instantly diverted.

'I do hope it is not bad news,' Aunt Camilla said, biting her lips and clasping her hands together in anticipation of impending disaster.

'That is hardly likely,' Lydia replied, but could not resist adding mischievously, 'unless there is an outbreak of the plague in town.'

She carefully broke the seal and unfolded the paper.

My dearest Lydia, she read, in papa's neat, uncrossed handwriting, *I trust that you are enjoying your stay with your Aunt Camilla – a charming woman, as I recall. I suppose that your mother and sister are well, although that is mere conjecture on my part. I never see them from one day to the next. They are forever attending a ball or ridotto or some such nonsense, and I only occasionally encounter them at breakfast. That may be the one blessing afforded me during this exile in town.*

Your mother and her cousin regale me with the tedious details of their enterprise, and it was thus that I learned of a most interesting occurrence concerning Louisa's presentation at court.

Here Lydia's attention was well and truly caught. Even

her own investigations were put aside as she read the tale recounted by her father. He had managed to catch a glimpse of his eldest daughter in her hoop and feathers before she departed for this auspicious event. The sight almost cast him into whoops, for he surely had never beheld anything so delightfully absurd. Nevertheless, he kissed her and told her how pretty she was. This, despite her attire, was nothing more than the truth. It was only later that he learned what had happened that evening in his absence.

'Is it very dreadful?' Aunt Camilla asked, making Lydia aware that she had been staring at the page before her with her mouth hanging open in astonishment.

'Absolute disaster,' she pronounced for her aunt's benefit.

'Is my sister no more?' Camilla asked faintly, her handkerchief covering her quivering lips.

'No, no,' her niece reassured her. 'It is merely my own sister's social standing which appears to be ruined.'

'What!' Camilla leaned forward, her megrims forgotten as she scented delicious scandal. 'Whatever has happened, child?'

'It seems,' Lydia said, her eyes taking in the words before her for the second time so that she did not misrepresent what her father had written. 'It seems,' she said again, 'that Louisa was to be presented at court.'

'How delightful!'

'Not so delightful,' Lydia corrected, with more than a tinge of satisfaction.

From what papa wrote, she gathered that all had gone quite well at first. Louisa was in very good looks and was admired by several persons of the first stare. However, it transpired that she had been too nervous to partake of food that day. The magnificence of the occasion, the heat of the candles in the brightly lit room, and the giddiness brought on by an empty stomach, proved to be too much for her. Upon meeting the Regent, she promptly smiled and swooned away in an inelegant heap at his feet.

'How mortifying!' Camilla cried, genuinely distressed.

'Listen to this!' Lydia could scarcely contain her mirth as she read aloud from papa's letter:

'The Prince, it appears, was much disconcerted by this performance and even though Mama produced her hartshorn, which instantly revived the poor girl, he avoided her pointedly for the rest of the evening. There were more than a few smiles hidden behind fans, and Louisa actually burst into tears after overhearing a witticism directed at her. They soon departed, and indeed have not left the house for the past two days.'

'It would have been better for her if she *had* died,' Camilla pronounced with a shudder.

'I fear she must give up her ambition to marry an earl,' Lydia agreed, trying to sound sympathetic.

'I beg your pardon?' Camilla was more mystified than ever.

'Never mind, aunt.' Lydia poured herself a cup of tea, her spirits miraculously revived despite her lack of sleep. 'No doubt she will make a reasonable match in spite of her *faux pas.*'

'I do hope so.' She did not sound at all hopeful, however.

'If she can but appear to advantage at some public function – at the theatre, or a private ball, perhaps – she may yet redeem herself.'

'Oh!' Camilla cried, instantly diverted from their discussion, 'I had almost forgotten: we, too, are invited to a ball, my dear.'

CHAPTER EIGHT

A CHANGE IN THE WIND

Mr Thomas Savidge had decided that he was risen to a high enough place of prominence in society that it was incumbent upon him to host a ball at the Golden Cockerel. He could not proceed, of course, without the express authority of Mrs Wardle-Penfield. Nor was that lady persuaded to sanction such an event without a good deal of cajoling and a subtle suggestion that the idea had been entirely her own from the beginning. In the end, she insisted upon planning the affair herself. It could not be denied that this was the simplest solution, which would do away with the inevitable criticisms she would have levelled at every aspect of the occasion had anyone else been permitted to make the arrangements.

All Diddlington was swept up in a whirl of frenzied activity in preparation for what promised to be the most dazzling function the inhabitants had seen for many a

71

year. Everyone was invited, it seemed. Everywhere that Lydia and her aunt went, the talk was of nothing else. The murder in Wickham Wood was all but forgotten, which certainly was a boon to Camilla. Her spirits, so much oppressed by the shadow of death, revived miraculously.

'In truth,' Mrs Wardle-Penfield told them when they met in the mercer's, 'I thought it a welcome distraction from the gloom into which everyone has been cast. Mr Savidge is a worthy man – and indecently wealthy, if his manners leave something yet to be desired. It is quite unexceptionable and will do us all the world of good.'

Even Lydia could not help but be infected by the festive spirit. She submitted patiently to her aunt's scathing assessment of her small wardrobe, and agreed to have one of Camilla's old ball gowns made over to fit her smaller frame. After an interminable session with the local dressmaker, all seemed in good train. However, as they left that good lady's establishment, they were surprised to be hailed by a passing pedestrian.

'It is Monsieur d'Almain!' Camilla was suddenly all a-flutter.

'So it is.' Lydia smiled in spite of herself.

The Frenchman doffed his hat as he approached and bid them a polite 'good-afternoon'.

'My niece is being fitted for a new gown,' Aunt Camilla stammered not entirely truthfully.

'Ah!' Monsieur d'Almain smiled knowingly. 'The famous ball.'

'Indeed.'

Conversation might then have ended, had not Lydia

taken it upon herself to learn a little more about this interesting gentleman. She had only glimpsed him upon
occasion since the night of Mrs Wardle-Penfield's card
party, and scarcely exchanged five words with him.

'Will you also be attending the ball, sir?' she enquired
artlessly.

'Yes indeed.'

'Mr Savidge tells me that you are an artist of some kind,
monsieur,' Lydia pressed him. 'Do you paint portraits?'

He laughed, a surprisingly youthful sound. 'No indeed,
Miss Bramwell. I am a designer of furniture, jewellery and
assorted pieces. I do not make the pieces myself, you see,
but only supply the designs for the artisans to produce the
final product.'

'How fascinating!' Aunt Camilla's eyes glowed with such
adoration that Lydia was hard put to it not to dissolve into
a fit of giggles. Her aunt obviously thought everything
about the man fascinating.

'I would have thought,' Lydia said honestly, 'that you
would have done better to work in London, sir.'

'I do not find London to my taste,' he explained. 'There
are many *émigres* there. Most of them look back to France
with longing. I wish only to forget the past and make a new
life for myself here in England: *La vie Anglais*,' he added,
his smile widening.

'I think you are very wise.' She was actually somewhat
surprised at his attitude.

'I have a great admiration for the English,' he told her.
'This is my home now, and I do not miss the other. As for
my work, Mr Bridge cares not where I live so long as my

work is satisfactory.'

'Mr Bridge?' she queried, startled. 'Of Rundell, Bridge and Rundell?'

'The very same.' He gave a slight bow. 'I work for the finest, you see – although some of my work has been for Green, Ward and Green, who are also on Ludgate Hill. But for Mr Bridge I have designed the snuffboxes, medals and more than one diadem for the Royal Family.'

Even with her limited experience, Lydia was aware that this unassuming gentleman dealt with the premier gold and silversmiths of England, who produced nothing but the best quality for their wealthy and titled patrons. While she did not share the awe felt by her lovesick aunt, she was impressed in spite of herself.

'You must be paid handsomely for such work, sir,' she exclaimed.

'Lydia!' Camilla was scandalized by the vulgarity of mentioning money so freely, turning apologetically to the Frenchman. 'Please forgive her, sir.'

'I am not in the least offended,' he reassured them both. 'I am indeed well paid. Well enough, at least, to hire a chaise to convey me to the ball on Friday. I wonder . . .' His pause was too enticing to resist.

'Wonder what, sir?' Camilla asked breathlessly.

'Would it be too forward of me . . .' he coughed slightly, as though he found it difficult to utter the words 'Would you do me the honour of allowing me to convey you to the ball?'

For a moment, Camilla Denton was quite bereft of speech. Had she seen Christ descending from Heaven with his angels, she could not have looked more rapturously amazed. It was left to Lydia to voice their acceptance.

'That would be wonderful, would it not, Aunt?' she said eagerly.

'Indeed.' Camilla swallowed and recovered herself enough to add, 'But we would not wish to impose upon your good nature, sir. . . .'

'I would consider it a pleasure – and a privilege – to escort two such charming ladies.'

So it was settled, and the two charming ladies made their way home. Camilla was in a state of euphoria quite out of proportion to the event, while Lydia was very pleased with herself for having discovered more about her aunt's suitor and having done more than her aunt had ever done to encourage his attentions.

They had almost arrived at the cottage when they were accosted by the Digweed sisters, who had their own confused speculation about the promised ball.

'Just a select company,' the eldest nodded sagely.

'Everyone in town will be there,' her sister insisted.

'Such a charming man.'

'Dreadful mushroom.'

'The weather sure to be fine.'

'Bound to rain.'

'Must have a bottle green domino made.'

'Russet the only colour for a cloak.'

'Is that not Mrs Wardle-Penfield?'

'Surely not, Honoria.'

'Must speak with her a moment.'

'Adieu!'

On the evening of the ball, Camilla herself arranged Lydia's coiffure in a much more simple style without the profusion of curls and ringlets too often favoured by damsels fresh from the schoolroom.

'I think it much more becoming,' she said, eyeing the results in a mirror.

Upon consideration, Lydia found herself in agreement. Her aunt might not be the brightest candle on the branch, but she had an unerring eye for fashion which her niece was coming to appreciate. The dress, too, was quite fetching. Of a pale golden colour, rather than the usual virginal white, with sleeves rather over-puffed, it made her look far less insipid than the gowns mama had made for her.

'Thank you so much, dearest aunt.' She gave Camilla a kiss of real gratitude. 'I have never looked half as pleasing before. Monsieur d'Almain will have eyes for no one but you, of course.'

'Hush, Lydia!' Camilla coloured and smiled in spite of her rebuke.

But Lydia could not deny that her aunt was especially lovely tonight. Her gown of blue and green taffeta set off her eyes and made her look like Venus rising from the waves. The look in the Frenchman's eyes when he arrived proved Lydia's prophecy to be correct. He could scarcely tear his gaze away from the vision of Miss Denton in all her finery. He was looking quite dashing himself, and even Lydia could understand her aunt's fascination, however ill-timed it might be.

It was a short but pleasant drive to the inn, which was ablaze with light. The high street was a clatter of carriages and a-bustle with a steady stream of arrivals. They were ushered into the main portal and directed along a corridor to a room at the rear of the building – the only chamber large enough to accommodate all the guests.

Pushing along beside her aunt through the crush, Lydia was surprised at the scene which awaited her. The room was lit by several large chandeliers and a number of sconces with crystal drops reflecting the light. Along the walls, a few narrow tables had been dressed with center-pieces of what appeared to be fresh spring flowers. On closer inspection, however, she realized that they had been cunningly fashioned from silk. At least they would not wilt in the heat of the many candles.

Mr Savidge and his son greeted the guests as they entered. The father was so full of pride in his accomplishment that he looked ready to burst. His son merely seemed mildly amused. However, when he spied Lydia's party, he frowned heavily. What was wrong with him? Lydia wondered, frowning in her turn.

It was some time before she had more than a polite word with John. He surprised her by procuring the first dance with her. In the event, he was prudent to have done so. Before very long, Lydia found that every dance was spoken for. She did not attribute this to the fact that she was in good looks tonight. There were so many gentlemen present that most of the ladies were able to pick and choose their partners at their leisure.

There was to be no waltzing, of course. Mrs Wardle-Penfield did not approve of the waltz, whatever the fine ladies of London might say. It most certainly would not do for Mr Savidge's ball, which must be held to the absolute strictest standards of propriety.

Some young ladies were disappointed when they learned of this, but it was no loss to Lydia. Unlike her sister Louisa, she had never bothered to learn the steps.

When John led her out onto the floor, she was more than happy. She saw Monsieur d'Almain partnering her aunt and knew the thrill of triumph. She herself was promised to him later in the evening, but she knew that he had asked her out of politeness. Besides, more than one speculative glance was directed at the handsome Frenchman and the staid Miss Denton. The town tabbies lapped up scandal broth like fresh cream, and they were sure to have their fill of it tonight.

'Who got you up in that rig tonight?' John demanded as they made their first steps.

'You do not approve?' she asked, startled at his tone.

He reddened slightly before replying, 'It is just that you are almost good-looking tonight.'

'In contrast to my usual hideous countenance?' she queried, feeling her anger rise.

'I did not mean that.' The movement of the dance drew them apart. Upon their reunion, he added, 'I just never thought of you as a proper young lady. That is all.'

'Well, how *did* you think of me?'

'I did not think of you at all.'

While Lydia did not generally consider herself to be 'missish', this was definitely not the kind of thing that any young lady longs to hear. Not that she considered John in the light of a suitor, but his patent indifference was not calculated to endear him to her.

'Well, you need not think of me again, sir!' she snapped. The dance ended and she stalked off in the direction of her aunt, leaving John standing in the middle of the floor with a curious expression on his face.

She studiously avoided him for the remainder of the evening. What should have been a very pleasant experience had been entirely spoilt, in any case, and she railed silently at the insensibility of the male sex.

'What is the matter?' Aunt Camilla asked her, seeing the distress writ on her face.

'Men are beasts!' Lydia answered in the time-honoured phrase of the maligned female.

'You have quarrelled with John?' The older woman correctly interpreted this remark.

'I would not call it a quarrel, precisely,' Lydia said. In fact, they had barely exchanged enough words for it to qualify as a genuine quarrel. But certainly their hitherto placid relationship had taken an unexpected and inexplicable detour.

Later that evening, after Monsieur d'Almain had deposited them ceremoniously at their door, Lydia heard even more disturbing tidings. She could see that her aunt was more than ordinarily nervous. Normally as silent as a preacher on a Monday morning, she had been peculiarly garrulous on the ride home. She chattered away about the difficulties of preserving blackberries, and the shocking way Mrs McBride's maidservant had behaved: a litany of trivial detail which bewildered the Frenchman as much as it did Lydia.

'What on earth is wrong, Aunt Camilla?' Lydia exclaimed as soon as the front door closed behind them.

'Oh Lydia!' To her consternation, the elder woman burst into tears. 'I would like to strangle Mrs Wardle-Penfield.'

'You would have to join a very long queue,' her niece commented. 'But what, in particular, has she done?'

'You know how she was certain that Monsieur d'Almain was somehow connected with the death of that poor man in the woods?'

'Yes,' Lydia answered grimly.

'Well,' Camilla sniffed loudly, 'she must have told *everyone* her suspicions, because they were all looking at him and whispering tonight. It was terrible!'

Lydia could have kicked herself. She had been so preoccupied, especially after her exchange with John, that she had not been as observant as usual. How could she have missed something so important? Now that she cast back in her mind, she *had* noticed that there was a great deal of talk tonight and some sly looks cast in the direction of her aunt and the Frenchman. She had put it down to speculation concerning their attachment, but it seemed that she was mistaken.

'I am so sorry, dearest.' What could she say to comfort the wretched woman?

'If he should be arrested, I shall die!'

This dramatic pronouncement was not as effective as Camilla might have hoped. Histrionics were entirely wasted upon her niece. However, it did provoke her to reply with some asperity that she could not imagine why anyone would arrest the man.

'There is no indication that he was involved in Mr Cole's murder.'

'You do not know the people in Diddlington.' Her aunt shook her head sadly. 'At least two people gave him the cut direct tonight. He will cease to be invited anywhere . . . he will be forced to leave the village in disgrace. . . .'

Lydia considered the matter, and realized that her aunt could well be right. Even if Monsieur d'Almain were never charged with the murder, a cloud of suspicion would surround him as long as the true murderer was not apprehended. And, with all due respect to John's father, Lydia was inclined to think that Mrs Wardle-Penfield had formed a fairly accurate opinion of his abilities. He was not the man for this job.

'We must do something,' she said aloud, more to herself than to her aunt.

'What can *we* do?' was the plaintive response. 'What can anyone do?'

'I will speak to John.'

'But you have quarrelled with John,' Camilla pointed out.

'I will make it up with him.' Lydia shrugged carelessly. 'It was no great matter.'

'That is not what you said earlier.'

'In such a case as this,' her niece said grandly, 'one must put aside petty differences for the sake of a higher cause.'

CHAPTER NINE

ADVENTURE AT LAST

In pursuit of this 'higher cause', Lydia scribbled a note to young Mr Savidge the next morning and enlisted the help of Charity to deliver it. The poor maid thought it monstrously romantic, and set out with the precious billet as soon as her duties allowed. The response was gratifyingly prompt. Indeed, he instructed the maid to wait while he penned his own lines. He offered his escort to both Lydia and her aunt, knowing that they were engaged to attend a musicale at Mrs Bitterwood's that evening. Naturally, Lydia accepted.

Though she itched for private conversation with him, Lydia was forced to endure a lengthy period in the carriage with her aunt as chaperon. They were rather late in arriving at their destination, and the performance had already begun. This entailed a further delay.

First Miss Jane Bitterwood sang a charming folk song in a perfectly dreary and uninspired soprano voice. As the daughter of their hostess (and the godchild of Mrs Wardle-Penfield), enthusiastic applause was an absolute necessity, of course. This was followed by a lively madrigal which garnered more genuine praise for the quartet of young people.

Finally, Miss Ophelia Scott commandeered the pianoforte and treated them to a truly remarkable rendition of a Scarlatti sonata. Lydia had never heard a solo performance which managed to sound so much like a duet in which both pianists were sadly inebriated. Miss Scott's right hand managed the treble clef tolerably well. However, her left hand seemed to have a will of its own. It meandered aimlessly up and down the bass clef like a lost lamb, tripping over flats and tumbling into sharps with wild abandon. Her audience, mercifully, was as incapable of recognizing her errors as it would have been of appreciating a more skilled performance. Lydia, who admired Scarlatti's complex compositions, reluctantly confessed to herself that she probably would not have enjoyed a correct interpretation half as well, although her lips were quite sore from the pressure of her teeth as she bit hard upon them to keep from laughing.

Indeed, she almost forgot her mission tonight, until John approached her and drew her aside under cover of the rapturous applause which followed.

He spoke quickly, an awkward apology upon his lips:

'I did not mean what I said yesterday, Miss Bramwell,' he stammered, his whole attitude quite at odds with his usual calm demeanour. 'Of course I think of you. We are friends, are we not?'

'*I* certainly thought so,' Lydia told him, rather enjoying his discomfiture. 'But there is no need to dwell on what happened last night. It is in the past now, and best forgotten.'

'I am glad,' he said, 'that you are so charitable. I feared that you would never speak to me again.'

'Nonsense!' She craned her neck to ascertain whether anyone might be attending to them. Thankfully, the others were all crowding around the musicians, praising and questioning as if they understood what they said.

'What is it that you want of me?' John asked.

'I need your help.'

'What is wrong?'

'There is still a great deal of talk about Monsieur d'Almain and the late Mr Cole.'

'I know.' John's face darkened and his mouth compressed. 'More than one person last night made it clear that they considered d'Almain to be *persona non grata*.'

'I want you to return to Wickham Wood with me.'

'Very well.' He did not pretend to misunderstand her. 'If we can prove that the smugglers were responsible for the murder, d'Almain's name will be cleared.'

'Tomorrow, then?'

'The next day,' he corrected her. 'I am engaged with friends tomorrow evening and will be out too late to accompany you.'

'Cockfighting?' She raised an eyebrow knowingly.

'Not at all,' he said with great dignity. 'Merely a convivial evening in Piddinghoe, where my grandmother lives. I have a numerous acquaintance there.'

'Can you not cry off?'

'I have no intention of doing so.'

'Not even for me?'

'Not even for you,' he said firmly.

'I shall go alone, then.' She raised her chin and stared defiantly into his eyes. 'I know the way now.'

'If you attempt anything so foolhardy,' he answered in a level voice, 'I shall put you over my knee and spank you!'

'You sound like my father,' she complained, hating to acknowledge that he was being perfectly sensible.

'Perhaps that is because you are behaving so childishly,' he replied, with the conscious superiority of one who was three years her elder.

In the end, she accepted the fact that their expedition must wait. At least they were on their usual friendly terms: or almost so. Something had changed, though she was not exactly sure what it might be.

When the day arrived, Lydia was more nervous than her aunt, checking the clock and starting at every sound. She told herself that she was being absurd. This was not the first time she had accompanied John on such an expedition. There was nothing to fear, was there?

Still, there was a feeling of intense relief when she finally escaped from the confines of the cottage that night and made her way to the same spot where she had met John before. Since their journey to the wood covered the same ground, descriptions are superfluous. The only difference was that the moon was no longer full, and so their vision was more limited than previously.

For some time their experience was drearily similar. Lydia was no longer disturbed by the strange night sounds, and was very nearly about to fall asleep once more when a sharp nudge from John's elbow alerted her that they were no longer alone in the woods. Almost simultaneously, she heard a rustling in the underbrush, as if a large animal were pushing its way unceremoniously through the trees. Dried twigs crackled beneath heavy boots and muted voices appeared to be carrying on patches of conversation. She almost squealed – not from fear but from sheer excitement – before common sense came to her aid and kept her silent.

There was a swoosh-swooshing sound, and Lydia saw two white, billowing objects sailing through the trees. A wailing sound accompanied them as they described a wide arc in the darkness. They certainly were not birds. Any one of the villagers would have sworn they saw a ghost; but with the knowledge that other humans were in the woods, Lydia knew that the explanation for these apparitions was a natural one.

A twinkle of lanterns through the trees made it fairly easy to spot where their quarry was at any time. However, it was as well that they were expecting them. A chance traveller, or an inebriated gentleman, would very likely have run like a rabbit in the opposite direction – which was probably the exact effect which they intended.

At one point the shadowy figures with their small lanterns were only two or three yards away from Lydia's and John's hiding place. They hunched low to the ground, knowing that if they were caught by these desperate men they might share the same fate as the late Mr Cole.

'D'ye see the entrance yet?' one of the men asked gruffly.

'Almost there, Ben,' his confederate replied.

'Nobody about tonight.'

'Wasted a bloody good show,' another said with a loud guffaw of laughter.

Then the voices faded, along with the lights. The stillness was suffocating.

'Shall we go now?' Lydia whispered.

'No,' John whispered back. 'They may return this way. We'll have to stay here until we're sure they're gone. And keep quiet,' he added unnecessarily.

John was correct in his surmise. About an hour later, another procession of lamps and voices passed by them in the opposite direction, heading out of the woods. Only when the last of them was well out of earshot did the two watchers rise from their cramped position on the woodland floor.

'Oh John!' Lydia cried at last. 'We were right: there *are* smugglers in the woods.'

In her excitement, she threw her arms around his large frame and hugged him tightly. Inevitably, he did the same. But as she looked up into his face, barely visible in the faint moonlight, she was quite unprepared for what happened next.

John bent his head and pressed his lips to hers in what was quite a tolerable kiss. Lydia was not certain what she should do. However, since she found the experience very pleasant, she returned it. Mama would almost certainly have considered it improper, though her daughter could not imagine why.

'Why did you kiss me?' she asked some time later, when they emerged from the wood.

'It seemed appropriate,' John said a little diffidently. 'Did you not like it?'

'I liked it very much,' she answered honestly. 'I was just surprised. That is all.'

'Would you mind very much if I did it again?'

'No indeed.'

He pulled her gently against him and repeated the previous exercise. This time she was prepared for it, and found it even more enjoyable than before.

'I think,' John said, raising his head, 'that it is best if we do not go into the woods alone together any more.'

'I quite agree.'

They arrived at the spot where John's horse was tethered and were soon riding back to town.

'I will inform my father of what we have discovered, and we will get some men to come down here and flush out the gang.'

'I wish I could be there!' Lydia cried, although she knew that this was impossible.

'It will be best if your name is not mentioned in relation to this matter,' John told her, frowning. 'My father would be quite scandalized – and rightly so.'

'Fustian!' Lydia protested. 'But I know what you mean. Aunt Camilla would doubtless swoon if she knew what we had been about tonight.'

Upon reflection, Lydia was not sorry that their adventure

had ended. While they were searching for the murderer of Mr Cole, they had developed a degree of camaraderie. They might almost have been brother and sister.

But although she had no brother, Lydia was very sure that one did not kiss one's brother the way she had kissed John. In fact, she had never had the least desire to kiss any man in such a fashion. However, she now found that she very much wanted to do so again: but only with John. This was most disturbing.

It was now that she understood John's remark at the ball. He said he did not think of her at all. What he had meant was that he did not *need* to think of her. She was simply there. She was his companion and fellow adventurer. She was his friend. There was no need to dwell on any feelings he might have for her. In truth, she had felt the same.

Things were no longer so simple. One might as well face the fact that she now saw John in a very different light: as an attractive young gentleman who might or might not play a significant role in her future happiness. It was obvious that his own thoughts were moving in a similar direction.

It occurred to her that she would very likely marry him. Thoughts of marriage had never entered her head before. She left such things to Louisa. How odd that her new acquaintance should have caused such a revolution in her thinking.

It was not that Mr Savidge was extraordinarily good-looking. His countenance was pleasing enough, and he had a fine figure. But there were other gentleman who could boast better features and more address. Yet she felt an affinity with him which was undeniable. She would not put a name to this feeling. She would not define it as 'love' without further cogitation and perhaps several more kisses.

Still, it was an interesting and unexpected development – an adventure in its own right.

CHAPTER TEN

SHOCKING DISCOVERIES

The next evening, Thomas Savidge dispatched a number of armed men to Wickham Wood. Not many of the residents of Diddlington were aware of this maneouvre, and most that did know were mystified as to its intent.

However, within twenty-four hours of this expedition, the news was everywhere: a gang of murderous smugglers had been apprehended in the wood. The praises of Diddlington's Justice of the Peace were upon everyone's lips. What genius! What foresight! What uncanny abilities (hitherto unsuspected) the man must possess! The invaluable contribution of his son and of Miss Bramwell were, of course, completely unknown to the general populace.

'Mr Savidge has certainly surprised me,' Mrs Wardle-Penfield confessed to Camilla and Lydia. 'I truly did not think he had it in him.'

'I would not doubt,' Lydia said demurely, 'that he had information from another source, which perhaps contributed to the success of his venture.'

'Indeed, I think you must be right.'

The saga of their battle with the bloodthirsty gang grew richer with each re-telling. From a dozen desperate men, the number of smugglers swelled to 'near 'bout a hundred'. The flesh-wound which one of Mr Savidge's men received became a mortal injury from which only the hand of Providence had saved the unfortunate fellow. It was therefore left to John – who had been present on the momentous occasion – to supply Lydia and her aunt with a more accurate account of the proceedings.

Lydia persuaded Aunt Camilla to invite both John and Monsieur d'Almain for tea one afternoon. It was some time before she could convince her timid relation that it would not seem at all *fast* for them to be entertaining two gentlemen in their house.

'Dinner, perhaps, might not be appropriate,' Lydia conceded. 'But tea can surely give offence to nobody.'

In the end, the two men were gratifyingly flattered at the invitation, and the four spent an enjoyable hour – or rather more – together. If tongues wagged afterward among the old tabbies of the village, that was only to be expected.

'You must tell me all about it,' Lydia insisted to John, referring to the apprehension of the smugglers.

'I would not wish to discompose your aunt, Miss Bramwell,' he protested.

Camilla had been gazing into the eyes of her other guest, but managed to adjust her attention – perhaps because d'Almain himself seemed very interested.

'I assure you, I shall not be at all discomposed,' she said graciously. 'Now that they have been apprehended, I feel that we may all rest easy in our beds at last.'

'I rested quite well *before* they were apprehended,' Lydia remarked, causing the gentlemen to smile while her aunt merely sighed at her lack of sensibility.

'We – that is, I,' John began with a sideways glance at Lydia, 'had determined that there might be some smuggling activity in Wickham Wood. I lay in wait on Tuesday evening, on purpose to discover whatever might be going forward there.'

He described pretty much what they had witnessed together, which Lydia already knew. She displayed far more interest when he continued to tell how he had informed his father of all he had heard and seen.

'Whatever did Mr Savidge say?' Aunt Camilla asked.

'At first,' John admitted, 'he thought it all a hoax.'

'He should have known you better than that, monsieur.' The Frenchman shook his head decisively.

'He certainly should have!' Lydia seconded this assessment.

'When I did manage to persuade him that it was no Banbury story,' John proceeded with his tale, 'it was almost worse. He told me I was a young fool, with no more sense than a billy goat.'

'Quite right, too,' Aunt Camilla concurred. 'Not that you were not monstrously brave and clever, but consider what could have happened. You might have been murdered by those cutthroats!'

'Possibly.' John shrugged, then went on with his story. 'In

the end, I helped him to organize a search party. From the direction we – I – had seen the lights moving that night, I had a fair idea where their hiding place was located.'

Armed with this knowledge, it had not taken long before they found the entrance to a cave, well hidden by rocks and bracken. The entrance was small, but opened into quite a large chamber, where boxes of smuggled liquor and other goods were stored. One fellow was posted just inside the mouth of the cave, but he was easily overcome by the men appointed as the executors of His Majesty's justice.

Once they had seized the lookout, half of them waited in the cave for the other members of the gang to arrive, while several others were stationed at points nearby to capture any who might try to escape through the woods. They had not long to wait. That evening, when the rest of the gang came to collect some of their loot, they were no match for armed men who had been warned what to expect.

'And none of them escaped?' d'Almain enquired, brows raised in surprise and admiration.

'Not that we are aware of,' John conceded. 'There may be other members of the gang who were not in the woods that night. No doubt we will learn more in time.'

'Have they confessed to the murder of Mr Cole?' Lydia could not forbear to ask, since it was the principal cause of this campaign, however little the others might be aware of it.

'No,' John answered curtly. 'Three of the men did, indeed, confess to the murder two years ago.'

'Who was the victim?'

'Apparently, one of their own.' John rubbed his chin,

looking around at them all. 'He had been found taking rather more of his share than was customary. It was an act of revenge.'

'But they deny any knowledge of this latest crime?' d'Almain queried, frowning.

'Exactly so.'

'They must be lying!' Camilla exclaimed, unable to consider any other possibility.

'What motive can there be for lying?' d'Almain asked reasonably. 'They will hang for one murder just as easily as for two.'

'Then we are back where we started!' Lydia cried, exasperated and perplexed.

'*Pardon?*' the Frenchman said in his native tongue.

'Miss Bramwell,' John explained, 'was convinced that the two crimes were connected, and that solving one would lead inevitably to the solution of the other.'

'It is certainly logical,' d'Almain admitted.

'But it appears to be false.'

'But that means . . .' Aunt Camilla's voice died away on a note of acute distress.

'It means,' d'Almain said with a bow, 'that the good people of Diddlington are still free to believe that *I* am the murderer of Mr Cole, even if I am not responsible for the death of the other unknown fellow.'

The other three hardly knew what to say. This was undoubtedly what they had all been thinking, but would hardly have dared to voice aloud in his presence. It was almost a relief to hear him acknowledge the fact.

'They are all fools!' cried Camilla, at which point

d'Almain reached across to clasp her hand and bring it ceremoniously to his lips.

'I know that you, *mon ange*, would never believe something so vile of me,' he said huskily.

Once again the others were speechless. Such an overt display of his partiality for Miss Denton was so very un-English, and not at all the thing. Lydia did not disapprove, but she thought it rather excessive, and suspected that John felt the same. Her aunt, meanwhile, was so overcome by emotion that Lydia expected her to either swoon or weep. However, she managed to exercise enough self-control to choke out something quite unintelligible which everyone simply accepted as her assent to the gentleman's statement.

'As a matter of fact,' John interrupted with a slight cough, 'I can tell you, in confidence, that the smugglers were asked whether they were acquainted with you, sir. They denied any knowledge of your existence.'

'Then we may be easy on that head,' Camilla said, eager to grasp at this straw – which Lydia was quick to break.

'Since they also deny any involvement in Mr Cole's murder,' she said, 'their lack of knowledge does not immediately acquit Monsieur d'Almain.'

'In the minds of many here, I am already guilty.'

This was unquestionably true, and it was on this unsettling thought that their tea, which had begun so promisingly, ended. The gentlemen took their leave, and the ladies took to their beds: Camilla with an attack of nervous exhaustion and Lydia with a mind already beginning to consider possibilities. For she was determined that the Frenchman should not be pilloried for something she had no doubt he would scorn to do.

CHAPTER ELEVEN

A SERVING OF SCANDAL-BROTH

The outcome of Lydia's reflections was one which was becoming most common: she determined to speak to John about them. Before she could accomplish this ambition, she was treated to further food for thought from an unexpected source. Mrs Wardle-Penfield paid them a brief visit, assuring them that she was merely 'dropping in' to see how they were getting on. It soon transpired that she was eager to learn about the visit of the two gentlemen, which had become the latest *on dit* in this Lilliputian society.

'Of course,' the *grande dame* pronounced smoothly, 'Monsieur d'Almain has such polished manners, one might almost mistake him for an aristocrat. No one can hope to rival the French in such matters, after all.'

Lydia clenched her teeth together, refraining with difficulty from making a cutting remark at this obvious lure. It was clearly impossible to sneeze in this village without someone proclaiming that there was an epidemic of the influenza.

'We had a most enjoyable afternoon, did we not, Lydia?' Aunt Camilla answered coolly. She was displaying more backbone lately, Lydia thought. If that was the Frenchman's doing, he was already a hero in her eyes.

'Most enlightening,' Lydia agreed. 'Mr Savidge told us all about the capture of the smugglers.'

'Indeed! I do not know what this town is coming to,' Mrs Wardle-Penfield bridled, preparing for an oration. 'Such goings-on have never been heard of here. Most of the men, I believe, were from other villages nearby, and yet you may be sure that they will all be clapped together and known throughout the nation as "The Diddlington Gang". Quite shocking!'

'It may be a real boon,' Lydia said brightly. 'There will doubtless be many a visitor at the Golden Cockerel, who is there for no other reason than to see the spot where the Diddlington Gang was apprehended.'

'We hardly want that class of visitor here.' The older woman looked as if the very idea made her ill. 'The leaders, no doubt, will be hanged, and the rest will end their days in Australia – a dreadful, wild place unfit for human habitation, by what I hear.'

'I do not know,' Aunt Camilla was inclined to think otherwise. 'I have always thought Australia a terribly romantic place: wild, perhaps, but no more so than America.'

'America!' Mrs Wardle-Penfield spoke the name as if it were hell itself. 'Another land fit only for felons and vile religious sects.'

'I own I should love to visit America,' Lydia said. Then, with her usual practicality, she added, 'Australia, I confess, is too distant. I fear the journey would be excessively tedious.'

By now they had strayed a considerable distance from their original topic, but the older woman was determined to direct the conversation back to where they began.

'Well, I am sure we owe the capture of these criminals to the efforts of Master John.'

'He is monstrous brave, is he not?' Camilla agreed, expressing genuine admiration. Lydia wondered if she would have applauded the bravery of her niece, had she known of the part she played.

'At least we will not now have to endure all this talk of ghosts and goblins in Wickham Wood,' Mrs Wardle-Penfield said with some satisfaction. 'I believe that they found several white sheets, along with various accoutrements for simulating spiritual phenomena.'

'You, of course, were never fooled by such cheap theatricals,' Lydia praised her, acknowledging her genuine good sense and giving credit where it was undoubtedly due.

'I should think not!' Their guest appeared affronted at the very notion. 'I place no more store in the supernatural than I do in Sir Hector's treasure.'

'Sir Hector's treasure?' Lydia could not allow this interesting reference to pass by unquestioned.

'Utter nonsense!' Aunt Camilla admitted, shaking her head and sharing a smile with her old acquaintance. 'More village tales, my dear niece.'

'Is there treasure hidden at Bellefleur?' Lydia asked, her

pulse beginning to quicken in spite of herself.

'So it has been rumoured these twenty years or more,' Mrs Wardle-Penfield concurred. 'But nobody takes such things seriously.'

'Perhaps they should,' Lydia answered, as much to herself as to the other two. 'Yes, perhaps they should.'

It was another two days before Lydia was able to see John. Aunt Camilla was feeling poorly, which was not an unusual occurrence, especially when she was fretting herself so dreadfully concerning Monsieur d'Almain. She was determined to rouse herself from her bed to fetch a headache powder from the local apothecary, but Lydia very kindly offered to go in her stead. After all, she said reasonably, the exercise would be most beneficial to her, and the poor maid was behind hand with the housework as it was.

What could be more reasonable? And, more importantly, what could be so convenient for her own plans? At last she might contrive to speak with John!

Off Lydia went, her steps light and quick. She first patronized the apothecary, concluding her business rapidly and setting out thence in the direction of the inn. She briefly acknowledged the greetings of her fellow pedestrians who were now all well acquainted with her. However, she did not linger to chatter but hurried on her way with a wave and a smile.

Preparing to enter the inn, she was almost knocked down by a lady in a morning-dress of cherry-red and a matching hat trimmed with deep purple plumage. She was very obviously one of the lightskirts kept by wealthy gentlemen who frequented the area, and it was equally plain that she considered herself superior to persons who had no such lucrative connections. Lydia made a mental note to ask John who the woman's protector might be. Her aunt would be horrified by the very idea, but she knew John would not mind.

As fate would have it, John was assisting his father that day with the inn's accounts. Mr Thomas Savidge was dealing with some work in the stables and John was closeted alone in the small office at the side of the building. He was plainly curious when Miss Bramwell was presented at his door, but not unhappy to see her.

'Can you spare a few minutes, sir?' she asked, very formally for the sake of the waiting manservant.

'Certainly, Miss Bramwell.' John was equally polite, motioning her to take a seat on the other side of the desk. 'Please do come in.'

'I suppose,' she said in a low voice as the servant retreated back to the entrance hall, 'it would not do for us to shut the door?'

'That would cause the kind of talk which I'm sure neither of us would wish,' John said. Nevertheless, he did get up and half-close the door, letting it stand perhaps six or eight inches ajar.

'I have been thinking,' Lydia began earnestly.

'I'm done for now,' John muttered, with his sudden impish smile.

'Do be serious,' she complained.

'What is it, Lydia?'

She fidgeted a little, hoping that he would not laugh at

what she was about to suggest. Even to herself it seemed unlikely. But one must proceed in some fashion, and this was the only avenue which presented itself to her at the moment.

'What do you know of Sir Hector's treasure?'

John scowled at her. 'To whom have you been speaking?'

'Mrs Wardle-Penfield told me about it.' She added, attempting to be just, 'I must say that she placed no faith in its existence.'

'Neither does anyone else.'

'Then where did the rumours originate?' she asked.

'Oh, they have been around since I can remember.' He leaned back in his chair and began to unfold the tale. 'Apparently the story stems from the fact that Sir Hector travelled extensively in his youth.'

'The Grand Tour?' She raised a brow knowingly.

'Rather more than that,' he said. 'Alexandria, Baghdad, Jerusalem: places which most white men have only heard of or read about in books.'

A year or two after Sir Hector's return from his mythic journey, there began to circulate a story that he had found a great treasure which he had brought back with him from the East. The exact nature of the loot was never disclosed. Some speculated that it was a fortune in jewels; others that it was a single ancient artifact, likewise encrusted with special stones – or perhaps magical properties.

'In the last years, when I have visited him,' John explained, 'Sir Hector has indeed spoken of his "treasure", but I can never be sure if he is in earnest, or whether he considers it a fine jest. He may even have been persuaded in his own mind that it *is* true, merely by the constant repetition of it over the years.'

'You say that he is very old, and something of a recluse?' Lydia persisted.

'Over ninety, I should say,' John agreed, eyeing her with a mixture of amusement and concern. 'You do not mean that you really do believe this old wives' fable, do you?'

'Why not?' she cried defensively. 'Stranger things have been known to occur. Why should he *not* have discovered a treasure in Timbuktu or some such place?'

'In the first place,' he pointed out, 'Sir Hector is a very wealthy man in his own right. What use is a treasure to him?'

'The rich,' Lydia said grandly, 'are never satisfied. However extensive their estate, they are ever eager to enlarge it.'

'There is some truth in that,' he acknowledged somewhat reluctantly. 'But what does this have to do with the murder of Mr Cole?'

'Ah!' she cried dramatically. 'That was what I am determined to discover, though I have my own ideas.'

'Which are?' He was irritated, she thought, tapping his fingers restlessly upon the desk where his unfinished accounts lay before him.

'What if,' she suggested, leaning forward and lowering her voice, 'Mr Cole had been Sir Hector's companion on his journey all those years ago?'

'Impossible!' John said scornfully. 'He would have been far too young at the time. Sir Hector could give him a good forty years! Neither is it likely that someone of Mr Cole's class would have been travelling with a peer, except in the capacity of a servant.'

This momentarily dashed Lydia's enthusiasm, but it quickly revived under the impetus of her imagination.

'Let us suppose,' she said after a moment's hesitation, 'that it was Mr Cole's father, or someone else of his acquaintance, who knew about the treasure. Perhaps this person and Sir Hector had stolen the treasure—'

'I do not believe it!' John protested. 'Sir Hector is of a pious – almost saintly – disposition. I find it hard to believe that he would steal anything.'

'However, you did not know him in his youth,' Lydia reminded him.

'True.'

'Will you at least consider the possibility of my conjectures?' she pleaded.

'And, supposing them to be valid,' he said with a very direct look, 'what do you intend to do about it?'

'I have not yet determined what course of action to take. But once I have . . .' she caught her lips between her teeth, uncertain how to continue, 'may I rely on your support?'

John rose from his seat and came around the desk. He reached out his hand to her and she stood at once, looking up into his eyes. If ever a man's eyes could be described as 'true', they were John's.

'You may always depend upon me, Lydia,' he said, gently but firmly.

He then bent his head and pressed a kiss upon her lips which was equally firm and gentle. However, this was not enough for Lydia. She promptly flung her arms around his neck and returned his kiss with such fervour that he had no choice but to respond in kind. It was very pleasant, but did not last for long; for, just as everything was progressing in a most interesting manner, they were rudely interrupted by a startled cry.

'Well!' The scandalized syllable was uttered from a few feet away.

Somewhat reluctantly, John released Lydia and they both turned to look through the aperture of the door which they had so conveniently left ajar. This opening was quite enough both to give their audience an excellent view of the scene they were witnessing, and to allow John and Lydia to perceive the identity of the witness to their embrace. It was none other than Mrs Wardle-Penfield herself.

CHAPTER TWELVE

TRICKS AND STRATAGEMS

'Oh!' was all that Lydia was capable of uttering.

'Mrs P!' John added, staring at the lady in horror.

'If you will both excuse me,' Mrs Wardle-Penfield intoned with awful politeness, 'I will be on my way. It is plain that you are both very busy.'

She would have turned and stalked off, had not John emerged from his temporary paralysis in time to forestall her. He stepped forward and opened the door, calling out to her in his usual tone of calm authority, 'Pray do not be so quick to leave us, ma'am. If you would but spare a minute, I can explain all.'

She had but half turned, and was no doubt eager to depart that she might waste no time in spreading the word that Camilla Denton's niece and the innkeeper's son were carrying on the most scandalous liaison right under the very noses of Diddlington's fine citizens. However, at these words she hesitated. On the one hand, she wished to display her distaste at such unseemly dissipation; on the other, she was eaten up with curiosity as to what possible story the lad could come up with. In the end, curiosity won the day.

'I am sure,' she said, turning back to the office and directing a piercing gaze at a red-faced Lydia, 'that you owe no explanation to me.'

Lydia was secretly inclined to agree with her, but realized that nothing less would serve to save them from public humiliation and disgrace.

'We are betrothed, ma'am,' John said baldly. Lydia had never been so near swooning in her life, but could not think of any better ruse herself.

'I have already sought my aunt's approval,' she rushed into speech, eager to support his statement.

'I have written to Mr Bramwell,' John added mendaciously, 'and only await his permission before the banns are called.'

Mrs Wardle-Penfield looked from one to the other, eyes narrowed, and Lydia was aware of feeling unusually nervous. The old woman was no fool. But when she spoke, her words startled them both.

'You're a deal too young to be contemplating marriage, in my opinion,' she said. 'But you've both got heads on your shoulders, which is more than I can say for most young people nowadays, and I've seldom seen a couple better suited. You'll do.'

Having expressed her opinion on the matter, she obviously felt that there was nothing further to add. She said that the subject she had originally called to discuss was of no importance, and could wait. In the meantime, she must just visit the Misses Digweed. She left the happy couple to speculate on how soon the entire town would learn of their engagement.

'I am so sorry, John,' Lydia exclaimed as soon as they were alone again.

'I should not have kissed you,' he confessed grudgingly.

'It seemed a perfectly reasonable thing to do.'

'Did it?'

'Did you not think so?'

'It is certainly becoming a bad habit with me.'

'Kissing young ladies?'

'Kissing you.'

'You do not kiss other young ladies, then?' she asked, secretly rather pleased.

'I kissed Miss Carteret a few weeks ago.'

'Did you?' She was not so pleased at this news.

'Yes.'

'And did you enjoy it?' She was somewhat curious on this point.

'It was very pleasant,' he admitted.

'Oh.'

'But kissing you is more than pleasant.'

'Is it?'

'I should say so!'

'Still, it must be horrid for you to be forced to offer for me.'

'No.' He paused a moment before adding, 'To tell the truth, I had been considering offering for you for the past week or more.'

She stared at him in surprise. 'You said nothing of this to me.'

'Well, no,' he muttered. 'I mean, I wasn't sure what to do, so naturally I would not embarrass you so.'

'I see.' She did not, in fact. But what else could a young lady say?

'I suppose I must write to your papa,' John said.

'Perhaps it would be best if I wrote to him first.'

'If you think it best.'

'I do.'

'You had better inform your aunt,' he said with a wry look, 'before she hears it from one of her friends!'

'What!' Camilla Denton sat bolt upright in bed. The powders which Lydia had fetched from the apothecary were forgotten.

'I am betrothed to Mr Savidge,' Lydia repeated, and followed her news with a frank description of what had transpired today at the inn.

'Thank God John was willing to offer for you!' Camilla croaked, sinking back onto her pillows. 'Have you any idea how near you have been to total disgrace?'

'I have.' Lydia shrugged philosophically. 'But John would never allow my reputation to be ruined.'

'What were you thinking of, kissing him in such a wild fashion?'

'I very much enjoy kissing John,' Lydia replied. 'Why should I not?'

'Why not!' Her aunt looked as if she were about to expire in her bed. 'Unnatural child! Kissing can lead to . . . well, when you are married, you will find out what it leads to.'

'I imagined that there must be more to it than that,' Lydia confessed. 'I quite look forward to finding out what it might be. John says he likes kissing me much better than kissing Miss Carteret.'

Camilla closed her eyes, apparently abandoning the struggle to preach propriety to someone who was clearly out of her senses.

'John has made a noble sacrifice to save your virtue,' she said at last.

'Nonsense!' Lydia objected to this romantic excess. 'He would quite like to marry me, and I can think of nobody else *I* would prefer to marry.'

'You are in love with him?' Camilla asked, her eyes growing somewhat misty.

'I do not know.' Lydia cocked her head, considering the matter. 'I have never been in love before. How can one tell if one is in love?'

'One just *knows*,' Aunt Camilla said with simple faith in the mysterious powers of the human heart.

'Well I do not.'

'Then you are *not* in love.'

'Very well, then.' Lydia was not dismayed at this revelation. 'I am not. I must go and write to papa.'

She left her aunt with a look of complete bewilderment upon her pretty face. For herself, Lydia was not certain what she thought about 'being in love', as expounded by her aunt and so many others. It seemed an ephemeral condition at best, which scarcely survived a year of marriage. How many miserable love matches had she heard her mother speak of to her friends. In choosing a mate, it seemed to Lydia that the head had at least as much right to contribute to the decision as the heart. A little more common sense and a little less emotion was called for.

It took more than an hour for her to compose a letter to her father which managed to convey something of what had taken place, without alarming him unnecessarily. She reflected that it could not but be difficult for a daughter to announce that she intended to marry a young man she had known for only a few short weeks. Indeed, perhaps she *was* in love, for the most lovestruck young lady could hardly behave more idiotically.

Yet, in truth, she had not meant to consider marriage so soon. It had been, so to speak, thrust upon both of them: herself as much as John. Yet now that she thought about it, it had definitely been in the back of her mind. She really had meant to marry John someday, so why should it not be sooner rather than later?

She felt no common enjoyment of his company, and their thoughts often seemed to jog along remarkably well together. Except for his occasional lapse in kissing her without due caution (to which she had not the least objection), John had behaved just as a gentleman should do. She had better mention that to papa, she thought, writing swiftly: not the part about the kisses, of course, but only that Mr John Savidge was a most unexceptionable young man.

Should she exaggerate his fortune? No. Better not. It was more than respectable, in any case. Suddenly she began to laugh, for here she was writing of her expected marriage. She, who had come to Diddlington with no such thought in her head! It was so droll. What would Louisa say? And mama!

She went into such a fit of laughter that she collapsed on her bed, helpless and exhausted. Luckily, Aunt Camilla had heard nothing, so she was undisturbed. At length, she fell into a deep sleep from which she awoke the next morning completely refreshed.

CHAPTER THIRTEEN

UNEXPECTED DEVELOPMENTS

Before Lydia could post her letter the following morning, she received one herself. This was her father's latest installment in the story of Louisa's London season.

'Another letter, my dear?' Aunt Camilla was concerned. 'This will cost a fortune, I fear. Your allowance will never stand it.'

'Papa has got a friend to frank it, Aunt,' Lydia reassured her.

'What news?' the other lady could not refrain from enquiring.

'Another *débâcle*.' Lydia's head was bent over the page, the better to decipher her father's minuscule handwriting. He had clearly reduced the size of his script to save paper. 'Oh dear! I knew Louisa would make a cake of herself in that dreadful pink dress. With cherry-red ribbons too!'

She then went on to explain the famous argument over Louisa's attire. Camilla shook her head in wonder and disapproval, declaring at last that poor Louisa had even less sense than her sister. Lydia took no offence at this, knowing that almost every word and action on her part went against her aunt's strict notions of propriety.

Lydia read parts of papa's letter aloud to her aunt: enough to inform her that Louisa's appearance at an assembly in town had been greeted by universal derision. Even her hen-witted sister could not fail to notice the giggles hastily hidden by fans, nor the withdrawal of several ladies from her presence. She had, it seemed, gone home and treated her parents to a display of strong hysterics in which she blamed everyone for her disgrace: mama, Lydia – even poor papa, who had always maintained a safe distance from the proceedings connected with his daughter's come-out.

'It will be a miracle if she receives a respectable offer,' Camilla pronounced fatalistically.

'She never would listen to reason,' Lydia said, for the first time experiencing something like sympathy for her foolish and headstrong sister.

'I see,' Aunt Camilla nodded toward the sealed missive beside her niece, 'that you have your own news to dispatch. We had best go and do so at once.'

After a few minutes of bustle and confusion, they emerged from the cottage and made their way toward the centre of town. On the high street they were apprehended by the Misses Digweed, who clearly had been acquainted with all the pertinent (and impertinent) facts surrounding her engagement to Mr Savidge.

'Such wonderful news!' cried the elder.

'You know what they say about "marrying in haste",' the latter remarked.

'A nine-days' wonder!'

'Been expecting it this age.'

'So well-favored.'

'Plump in the pocket too.'

'Oh, Dorothea!'

It was some time before they were able to disentangle themselves from the verbal web of this enterprising duo. When they did so, Lydia was surprised to find her aunt hailing a complete stranger.

'Kate!' Miss Denton called out to a short, plump young woman who had just stepped up onto the pavement perhaps three yards ahead of them. 'It *is* Kate, is it not?'

'Yes, Miss Denton,' the young woman replied, dropping a slight curtsy to them both.

'It has been a long time since we have seen each other. Just before Easter, I believe?'

'Yes ma'am.'

Aunt Camilla introduced Lydia to the young girl, adding that she was a servant at Bellefleur.

'How does Sir Hector get on?' Camilla added, with real concern. 'Such a fine old gentleman!'

'He's been very poorly these past weeks,' Kate responded, shaking her head sadly. 'Not at all himself.'

'Has he seen Doctor Humbleby?'

Kate replied that he had not.

'Really, Mrs Chalfont should have insisted upon it.'

'Mrs Chalfont?' Lydia asked curiously.

'Sir Hector's housekeeper that is, miss,' Kate enlightened the other girl.

'Is Sir Hector as ill as that?' Lydia began to probe gently, dangling her question in the hope of catching something worthy of her efforts.

'I've never known 'im to be so low, and that's a fact.'

'Perhaps,' Lydia suggested, 'all the trouble in Wickham Wood has overset his nerves.'

'Could be, miss.' Kate considered this explanation, which apparently found favour. 'Now that you mention it, this spell come on just around the time that man was found dead in the woods.'

'I think I should pay a visit to Bellefleur,' Aunt Camilla said, as if she had read her niece's mind. 'I shall bring along some brandy and a receipt for a tonic which is said to do wonders for persons of advanced age.'

'A splendid idea, Aunt.' Lydia's mind was returning to the problem with which she had been so consumed before her unexpected betrothal. 'I would love to meet Sir Hector. Perhaps he needs the company of a young person to lift his spirits.'

'Not likely you'll be allowed to see him,' Kate said sourly.

'I beg your pardon?' Even Camilla was startled at this piece of news.

'Sorry, ma'am,' Kate answered, looking somewhat shamefaced. 'It's just that Mrs Chalfont and Mr Tweedy—'

'Mr Tweedy?' Lydia asked, more mystified than ever.

'That's Sir Hector's valet, miss.'

'Oh.'

'Sir Hector,' Kate continued, 'won't allow nobody but Mr

Tweedy and Mrs Chalfont to see him. I think he's gone barmy, meself.'

'Oh, do not say so!' Camilla's distress was genuine. 'Such a dear, kind, Christian man.'

'It's as true as the Gospel, ma'am,' the young maid insisted. 'He just ain't 'imself.'

'I think we must see for ourselves, dear aunt,' Lydia insisted. 'We will call at Bellefleur tomorrow, and see what we can learn.'

'But if we are not permitted to see—'

'Perhaps he will be better by then,' Lydia said, refusing to be put off. Then she added to the servant, 'There is no need to mention this to anyone, Kate. We will surprise Sir Hector. Who knows but what he may be persuaded to see us after all?'

That evening John called to see them. Aunt Camilla, after expressing her best wishes to him, diplomatically withdrew. It was quite the thing for engaged couples to be permitted time alone together, and this particular couple could be most fatiguing. It was better for her nerves if she knew as little as possible of what transpired between them.

'Have you written to your papa?' John questioned Lydia as soon as her aunt left the room.

'Yes indeed. But John, you have not heard the latest news!'

'Are you engaged to someone else?' He smiled a little crookedly at her.

'Do not be a goose.'

She then related to him all that Kate had told them

119

earlier in the day. He listened intently, but apparently did not reach the same conclusion.

'I suspect,' she declaimed, 'that the old man is consumed by guilt. He murdered Mr Cole. . . .'

John laughed, which Lydia found extremely irritating.

'How did he do that?' he asked her.

'He overpowered him. . . .'

John laughed even more loudly.

'What do you find so amusing?'

'The image of a man of ninety-five years or more "over-powering" a healthy fellow almost half his age!'

'It is possible,' Lydia said with great dignity.

'But highly unlikely,' he replied, unconvinced.

'Very well!' she cried, thoroughly offended now, 'if you refuse to listen to me, you can go back to your inn, John Savidge. Good-night.'

With that, she swept from the room in a fine display of dudgeon. She was fortunate that she had been standing with her back to the door and was able to make a swift exit along the passage and up the stairs. Although she heard John calling her name as she ascended, she refused to heed him but went up to her room and left him to find his own way out.

How dare he laugh at her! His own fiancée! Well, she would show him. She would solve the riddle of Mr Cole's murder and bring Sir Hector (whom she had already cast as his murderer) to justice. Then he would acknowledge her superiority of mind and be forced to apologize for his unpardonable behaviour.

CHAPTER FOURTEEN

AN ILLUMINATING VISIT

The weather had grown considerably warmer, and the walk of four miles to the gates of Bellefleur was an unexpectedly pleasant excursion. For the most part they went at a brisk pace, only pausing now and then for the elder of the two women to rest momentarily. There had been no rain for several days, so there was no fear of mud and they had left their pattens at home. The lanes were not so dusty yet as they would be at the height of summer.

They crossed a pretty little stone bridge with a low wall which spanned a narrow brook running along the edge of the extensive property, and it was not long before the great stone pile rose magically before them as they ascended a sloping stretch of grassy ground.

'Here we are!' Lydia sang out gaily.

'Not quite,' Aunt Camilla said a little breathlessly. 'I am getting too old for such jaunts!'

'Do not be silly.' Lydia linked her arm with her aunt's and

they began walking up the drive to the front door. 'You have enjoyed this every bit as much as I have.'

'I do not know that I would go *that* far.' Camilla looked at the young girl with a degree of speculation. 'I do not know why you must needs visit Sir Hector, but since you are so determined I thought it best not to wait.'

'If the man is as ill as Kate described,' Lydia observed as they approached the front steps, 'there may not be much time left for me to meet him.'

To this Camilla made no reply. They knocked loudly at the door, which was soon opened by an elderly retainer who looked to be scarcely in better condition than his master.

'Good-morning, Mattucks,' Camilla greeted him pleasantly. 'My niece, Miss Bramwell, and I have come to pay our respects to Sir Hector. I would have brought her sooner, but understood that his health is not the best.'

' 'Morning, ma'am,' Mattucks wheezed at her before turning ever so slowly to bestow the same courtesy upon Lydia. 'I'm afraid the master still ain't up to seeing visitors. I'd best ask Mrs Chalfont.'

He directed them to a large open chamber which appeared to be more of a reception hall than a drawing room. Bellefleur was a Jacobean building, large and incommodious, with protruding wings on either end recalling the style of the homes in the reign of Elizabeth I.

Lydia's eye wandered to the fireplace, with an enormous mantel, above which was an elaborate carving of a heart surrounded by swirling acanthus leaves and surmounted by a flame out of which rose a crucifix. The family, she supposed, must have been of the Roman Catholic faith.

Even so, she would have expected their coat of arms to have pride of place rather than this odd religious symbol.

'What do you make of this, Aunt?' she asked, looking up at it and reading the simple letters and numerals carved immediately beneath in small but deeply incised script: 'P.S. one-one-nine-one-one.'

'You know, I had never noticed the writing beneath the heart,' Camilla said, screwing up her face in an effort to see it better. 'It reminds me of something, but at the moment I cannot recall what it is.'

'It *is* an unusual piece, is it not?'

They both turned around in unison at this. The speaker was a tall – some might say Junoesque – woman in a plain gown and a lace cap. She was not young. Indeed, Lydia imagined that she must have more than forty summers behind her. Yet she was still strikingly attractive. There was a force of personality about her too. She had a presence that was wasted as a housekeeper. She should, Lydia thought, have been on the stage.

'I could not help admiring it, ma'am,' Lydia admitted.

'Good-day, Mrs Chalfont,' Camilla Denton said.

There was the usual awkward interval of introduction before Mrs Chalfont was able to inform them that their effort today had been wasted.

'It was kind of you to come so far,' she said graciously, 'but I fear it may be some time before poor Sir Hector is able to receive visitors.'

'Has he no family, ma'am, who comes to see him?' Lydia asked, trying to glean as much information as possible.

'There is a distant cousin in America,' the housekeeper

acknowledged, 'who will inherit the estate when Sir Hector has gone on to his reward.'

'That is too bad.' Lydia sighed and cast her gaze around the beautifully furnished room. 'I suppose it will be sold off to strangers.'

'I fear you may be right, Miss Bramwell.' Mrs Chalfont rose from her chair. 'But since you have come so far, perhaps you would like to see some of the house and grounds?'

'I would not wish to intrude, ma'am,' Lydia said so demurely that her aunt cast her a look of considerable surprise.

'It is no trouble at all, I assure you.'

She immediately began a practiced speech which she had doubtless delivered many times, conducting the two women through what seemed to be miles of corridors covered with imposing portraits and classical busts. She carefully avoided the portion of the house where Sir Hector was laid up in bed, explaining that he was sensitive to the least noise.

'Only myself and Mr Tweedy, his valet,' she elaborated, 'ever enter his bedchamber now. Anyone else brings on a nervous collapse.'

At length their tour led through the kitchens, where Lydia spied Kate and a younger housemaid passing through on their way to another room. From the kitchens, their path led them outside into a walled garden which was oddly unkempt, parts of it appearing to have recently been dug up for planting. Aunt Camilla volunteered to help Mrs Chalfont cut flowers to display on the tables inside. The sun was shining brightly, and Lydia very quickly decided to feign a headache brought on by the heat. The response of her two companions was immediate and most solicitous.

'Let us return to the house then, my dear. You may lie down upon a sofa until it is time for you to return.' Mrs Chalfont was all consideration. 'I shall even have the carriage fetched for you. I know Sir Hector would wish it.'

'This is most strange.' Aunt Camilla could not conceal her puzzlement. 'You are in general so healthy. I have never known you complain of the headache before.'

'I fear that the exertion of our walk. . . .'

'But you said that you found it so refreshing.'

This was not the sort of thing which Lydia desired her aunt to remember, and still less did she wish her to point it out to the housekeeper.

'I have tried to do too much,' Lydia said faintly. 'But pray do not fetch the carriage, and do not think of abandoning your cuttings on my account. I shall be quite well if I am left alone for awhile.'

'But you may become lost, my dear.' The housekeeper was smiling but insistent. 'Bellefleur is a large house, after all.'

'I shall ask one of the servants to direct me,' Lydia attempted to pacify her. 'I would only be more anxious if I felt that I had spoilt your own pleasure, and that of my aunt.'

'Very well, then,' Mrs Chalfont agreed reluctantly. 'But I shall at least accompany you to the kitchen and arrange that someone looks in on you to be sure that you are not too ill.'

'Thank you, ma'am,' Lydia said, attempting to look wan. 'You are all kindness.'

As it happened, it was Kate whom Mrs Chalfont directed to attend to Miss Bramwell. This was just what Lydia had prayed for.

Lydia found her way back to the drawing-room where their tour began, and arranged herself artistically on one of the sofas in case someone should come in unexpectedly. She was tempted to venture above stairs to Sir Hector's chamber, but the possibility of being caught held her back. It could be dangerous, and would certainly be embarrassing for herself and her aunt. They might be barred permanently from Bellefleur. In the end, she waited for perhaps ten minutes before Kate peered through the doorway.

'Are you all right, Miss Bramwell?' the girl asked her in a loud stage-whisper.

Lydia popped up from the couch so promptly that she startled the poor maid.

'I am perfectly well,' she said, beckoning for Kate to come forward. 'It was merely a ruse to give me time to speak with you.'

'You're very clever, miss!' Kate was lost in admiration at such resourcefulness.

'Tell me more about Sir Hector and what is going on in this house.' Lydia was whispering too, her gaze wandering toward the door to ensure that they were not overheard.

'It's just like I said before, miss.' Kate seemed mystified by Lydia's persistence, and uncertain what she should answer. 'Nobody but Mrs Chalfont ever goes in to see the master anymore. Although—'

To Lydia's surprise, a tide of red rose in Kate's cheeks. She caught her lips between her teeth and it was plain that she was afraid to say more.

'You may speak freely to me, Kate,' Lydia said sympathetically. 'I will not betray you if you have done something you ought not to have done.'

'If Mrs Chalfont ever knew,' the girl began, but Lydia was eager to assure her that no one would ever hear it from *her* lips.

'It was less than a sennight past, miss,' Kate whispered nervously. 'I was passing near Sir Hector's chamber when I heard a noise.'

'What kind of noise?'

'It sounded like something fell down, miss. I didn't know what to do.' Her hands were clenched in her lap and she looked down at them with something like shame. 'I know I shouldn't have gone in there, but I thought to myself, what if 'e's 'ad a fit or something?'

With no time to think, Kate knocked briefly before entering the room. It was very dark and gloomy, the rich satin curtains drawn to shut out the sun. She could clearly perceive, however, a figure lying in the bed, the arm hanging over the side. There was an empty glass on the floor beside the bed. This must have been what she heard falling upon the rug.

'Are you all right, sir?' Kate called out softly.

The next thing she knew, an arm reached across and snuffed out the single taper burning on a small table beside the bed, and a hoarse voice shouted at her, 'Get out, you stupid little slut! Go away and leave me to die in peace.'

She did as she was told, of course. A good servant always does. But the incident left her puzzled and uneasy. There was something about it, she confessed, that just wasn't right.

'Something was not right?' Lydia repeated, trying to follow the girl's train of thought.

'Well,' Kate considered the matter and attempted to put her thoughts into words, 'I know the master never spoke to me like that in the three years I've been in service here. But it wasn't that. . . .'

'Then what?'

But whatever it was proved elusive. Kate shook her head and declared that it was sure to come to her. Maybe if she had a good night's sleep, the answer would come to her in the morning. With that, Lydia had to be content.

'Very well,' she said, leaning back on the sofa. 'But as soon as you recall what it is that's troubling you about it, please let me know at once.'

'I will, Miss. I promise.' Kate stood up. 'I'd best be getting back to work now, before I'm taken to task for idleness.'

She walked toward the door and put out her hand to close it behind her. Then, quite suddenly, she stopped and stared at the handle she was holding and turned around to face Lydia. Her face was illuminated like some prophetess who had just received a divine revelation.

'I remember now!' she cried with obvious excitement. 'It wasn't his hand, miss. Indeed it wasn't.'

Before Lydia could respond to this, to seek enlightenment, a figure appeared behind the maid and a voice spoke so sharply that Kate started violently and grew as pale as a babe's christening gown.

'What are you doing here, Kate?'

'I'm so sorry, Mr Tweedy,' the poor child stammered, quite flustered at his unexpected appearance. 'I was just checking on Miss Bramwell. Mrs Chalfont asked me to.'

'Well, get back to your duties,' Mr Tweedy snapped. 'The young lady looks perfectly well to me.'

'Indeed, sir,' Lydia agreed, standing and walking towards them, 'I am completely recovered and think I will rejoin Mrs Chalfont and my aunt.'

The valet stepped back so that she could pass by him on her way to the garden. A forbidding-looking frown marred his somewhat bland features. He neither spoke nor smiled, but stared down at her with dark, suspicious eyes.

'Do not dawdle now, Kate,' he called out to the maid, who was several paces ahead of Lydia.

The two young women reached the kitchen at almost the same moment. Cook was in the midst of preparing for supper, and told Kate to mind her work did not fall behind.

'Will you be at church on Sunday?' Lydia asked Kate quickly.

'Yes, Miss Bramwell. Of course I will.'

'We will speak more about this then.'

Lydia considered that she had done very well for one day. For her part, Aunt Camilla was shocked at her behaviour. Being better acquainted with her niece than Mrs Chalfont was, she had come to the belated conclusion that her so-called illness had been no more than a performance put on for the benefit of the housekeeper.

'I was mortified!' Camilla cried as they walked back toward town later that afternoon.

'Oh, pooh!' was Lydia's considered response. 'What do I care what Sir Hector's housekeeper might think? Not that I suppose she suspected anything. Why should she? I am quite a good actress, I think.'

Camilla could not view the matter in so charitable a light, however. She remonstrated with the young girl for several minutes before she finally conceded the futility of further effort.

Meanwhile, Lydia decided to discover from her aunt whatever could be gleaned about those who were employed at Bellefleur. She was particularly interested in Mr Tweedy, whose menacing presence had so dismayed Kate.

Mr Tweedy, it seemed, was the nephew of Sir Hector's first valet. He had taken up the position upon his uncle's demise and had already been with Sir Hector for almost twenty years. Mrs Chalfont had been at Bellefleur for perhaps five or six years – Aunt Camilla could not recollect exactly. She was a widow, originally from London. A fine figure of a woman, although she gave herself such airs that some people (notably Mrs Wardle-Penfield) were not enamoured of her. It was said that Mr Tweedy had at first been very much against her, because she quickly came to have such influence over his master. However, it seemed that the housekeeper had managed to charm the valet as well, and it was even rumoured – not that Camilla believed a word of it, of course! – that they were rather more than friends.

As for the rest of the servants, the cook had been there for many years, and the young maids all came from respectable families in the village or the surrounding country. The butler, Mattucks, was almost as old as Bellefleur itself, and many of the young people joked that before that he had been employed by Noah on board the Ark.

It was all rather commonplace, Lydia supposed. But she could hardly wait to speak with Kate on Sunday. What she said might mean nothing, or it could be of the utmost importance.

Perhaps John could help her to make some sense of it. She longed to talk to him about it, but then remembered that they had quarrelled again. Well, she would not be the one to go crawling to him! The quarrel had been of his own making. Let him come to her, if he cared to do so.

A suspicion entered her mind that she was being very childish and silly about this, but she refused to heed it. She began to wonder if marrying John was really so sensible a plan as it had first appeared.

CHAPTER FIFTEEN

DEATH RETURNS TO DIDDLINGTON

It did not take very long for John to call upon his betrothed. He did not come alone, however. His father accompanied him, and it was plain that he was not as enthusiastic about his son's choice of bride as either John or Lydia would have wanted.

'I wish you both every happiness, my dear child,' Mr Savidge said to Lydia. He shook her hand, which did not bode well, Lydia thought. Thomas Savidge was the kind of man who would have been more likely to crush her in a hearty embrace if the match had met with his approval.

'I – I shall try to be a good and – unexceptionable – wife to John,' Lydia stammered, for once put out of countenance.

'I am sure you will be, child,' her future father-in-law smiled somewhat mournfully. 'Not but what I had higher ambitions for my son.'

'Miss Milbridge?' John enquired laconically. 'You were wasting your time and hers, if you thought I'd ever offer for that platter-faced ninny.'

'Miss Milbridge,' the elder Savidge said, 'is a fine young woman, and her family is very well-connected. Her cousins are related to the Duke of—'

'It would not matter to me if she was related to the Emperor of China,' his son answered with what the father clearly considered to be an appalling lack of respect. 'Nothing would induce me to marry her.'

'Well, there are other young ladies. . . .'

'I am to marry Lydia,' John said with finality. 'That is absolutely settled, and I think it most impolite of you to be mentioning any other plans you might have had at such a moment.'

'Forgive me, Miss Bramwell,' Thomas said with a slight bow. 'You are, of course, a charming young woman, and I'm sure will make my son very happy.'

'But I am not your first choice,' Lydia lamented, deciding that she would enjoy the man's discomfiture as much as possible. 'I quite understand, sir. I am a nobody.'

The older man produced a look of pained surprise, saying, 'I would never say such a thing to you, my dear.'

'But you think it.' She shook her head sadly. 'Naturally you must think so. After all, your son could have his pick of the young ladies around Diddlington, and to be entrapped by a mere Miss Bramwell. . . .'

'Entrapped!' John cried.

'Entrapped!' his father echoed with greater volume. 'I am sure—'

'I know I behaved shamelessly,' Lydia interrupted him once more, while John began to grin at her comic performance. 'Setting my cap at him in such a way . . . I do not know what can have possessed me, sir.'

'Well, he's a fine catch, my John.' Mr Savidge preened like the cockerel for which his inn was named. 'One can hardly blame a girl for—'

'For the Lord's sake, papa,' his son cut short his improper utterance, 'pay no heed to Lydia's Banbury stories. She is roasting you, sir.'

Thomas Savidge started, staring at the young lady in disbelief. It was beyond his comprehension that anyone could make a May game of him – and certainly not a chit of a girl, even one who had been elevated by a betrothal to his son. He dismissed John's words and bent an indulgent look upon Lydia.

'Well, well,' he said heartily, 'you are obviously a young lady who is up to every rig, and I suppose my boy could have done worse for himself.'

'Thank you, sir,' she answered demurely. 'I promise you that I will try to be a credit to the name of Savidge.'

John gave a snort of mirth. 'I don't doubt that you will,' he said, 'depending on how you spell it.'

'What do you mean by that, son?' his sire asked, never suspecting a jest.

'Nothing, sir,' his dutiful son answered, then added with the air of someone who had produced an unanswerable argument, 'But I have it on the authority of no less a personage than Mrs Wardle-Penfield herself that Lydia and I are very well suited and will assuredly make a go of our marriage.'

Had he produced a revelation from the sacred scriptures

themselves, he could not have so completely reconciled Mr, Savidge to the match. He now treated Lydia to the hearty but embarrassing embrace he had withheld at the outset and, after congratulating his son on his good sense, he very properly left them alone together.

Here was Lydia's opportunity to acquaint her beloved with the details of her visit to Bellefleur. He must have realized that argument was fruitless, and listened patiently to her recital.

'You must acknowledge now, John,' she concluded, 'that something is amiss at the home of Sir Hector.'

'It would seem so,' he replied cautiously. 'I would be very interested to hear what the maid has to say.'

'Kate?' Lydia nodded emphatically, in perfect agreement with him. 'I own that I never looked forward to attending church with such anticipation. Not that the vicar is not a fine preacher in his way, but I can hardly wait to hear what else Kate has to tell me.'

'In three days,' he said, affecting an air of ominous mystery, 'all will be revealed!'

'You may jest as much as you like.' She drew herself up with great dignity. 'But you will soon see that I am right.'

'Forgive me, Lydia.' He reached out and took her hands in his. 'I am willing to admit that there is more here than I had first supposed. But I beg you, in future, do nothing without first consulting me.'

'I do not intend to ask your permission for anything,' she protested. 'We are not married yet, after all.'

'It is not my permission,' he said gently, 'but my protection which I hope you will seek.'

'Your protection?' For once she was mystified.

'I believe I have that right, love.'

'From what do I need to be protected?'

He was in deadly earnest now as he looked straight into her eyes.

'If what you suspect is true,' he reminded her, 'then someone at Bellefleur has already committed murder at least once. You may be putting yourself in greater danger than you realize.'

This had, in all honesty, not occurred to Lydia before. If Sir Hector, or someone else, had not hesitated to kill before, why should she be immune? Suddenly she shivered, at which John drew her into his embrace. This was an unlooked-for pleasure, she thought. Really, had she known he would do such a thing, she would have shivered before this.

'I promise not to proceed any further,' she told him solemnly, 'if you will promise not to laugh at my speculations in future.'

'I swear it!' he cried, 'And thus I seal my vow.' Naturally, he kissed her. Just as naturally, she returned his kiss.

'One of the benefits of being engaged,' he said when at last he raised his head, 'is that I may kiss you as often as I choose.'

'I'm sure,' she quizzed him, 'that Mrs Wardle-Penfield would not agree.'

'At least her approval of our engagement has helped reconcile my father to the match.'

'Your papa is such a zany!' she exclaimed.

'It was wicked of you to tease him so,' John chided her, though with a glint of sympathetic humour in his eyes.

'I hope my own father will be as easy to persuade!'

'My knees knock together at the thought of his response to your letter.'

'It will not be many days before we know in what spirit he receives it.'

So they parted. Lydia considered that, although they might quarrel often, their arguments were quickly forgotten and their reconciliations were quite delightful.

In the course of the next few days, Lydia and John were quizzed and questioned endlessly on the subject of their betrothal. It was, she supposed, a welcome diversion after the events of the previous weeks. A wedding was a much more comfortable source of gossip than murder and armed ruffians in the woods.

And so, although she was anxious to meet with Kate on Sunday morning, the time passed more swiftly than she had anticipated. Before she well knew it, she was fastening her straw bonnet and walking arm-in-arm with Aunt Camilla to the small church but two streets away from their cottage.

The church was a fine old building, with a thatched roof and rounded apse. Some said it dated to before the Conquest; others placed it just after the advent of the Normans. In either case, it was a place of historic as well as spiritual significance, and a source of pride to the parish and the inhabitants of Diddlington.

A goodly number of people were gathered together as the

two ladies entered, but, although Lydia craned her neck in every direction, there was no sign of Kate. She sat through the service in a kind of dazed distraction, constantly turning around at the slightest sound, in hopes of seeing the young girl.

At last the final anthem was sung and the benediction uttered. The congregation began to file out. Lydia was conscious of acute disappointment. What had become of the maid? Had she been taken ill? Perhaps she had not been permitted to leave Bellefleur.

They stepped out into the sunshine, the green grass around them dotted with gravestones, and Lydia and Camilla were just about to engage John and his father in conversation when a rather noisy diversion occurred.

A young village boy named James Tredwell dashed onto the lawn, flushed and out of breath.

'Mr Savidge, sir!' he cried. 'Come quick, sir!'

'What is it, James, my lad?'

'It's Kate Eccles!' the boy gasped out, his big blue eyes seeming almost to pop from their sockets. 'She's dead, sir!'

CHAPTER SIXTEEN

A RARE HUBBLE-BUBBLE

They found her sprawled like a discarded doll behind a hedge in the gardens at Bellefleur. She had been strangled with a length of twine of the kind commonly used to secure parcels. In her Sunday best dress, she must have been on her way to church when her killer had surprised her – perhaps springing from his hiding place behind that very hedge.

All this Lydia and her aunt learned later that day from John. The moment the innkeeper heard the news, he had rushed off to the scene of the murder. John excused himself from his fiancée and her aunt, who accepted his departure without demur, and took himself off in pursuit of his father.

The small band of parishioners left standing by the church was silent for almost a minute as they watched the departing figures on their way to the great estate. Then, as if released from a magic spell, they all began to babble almost incoherently. Everyone expressed their shock and grief over yet another instance of violent evil in their midst.

'I cannot conceive,' Mrs Wardle-Penfield managed to project her voice above the hubbub, 'what reason anyone could have for killing poor young Kate.'

'It is so dreadful,' Aunt Camilla said faintly. 'And it was but three days ago – or was it four? – that we were there at Bellefleur ourselves.'

'It seems,' the vicar said, wringing his hands in great agitation, 'as though the Devil himself has come amongst us, having great wrath.'

'No doubt Satan has his share of disciples in every parish.'

This last was spoken by old Mr Jurby, the apothecary, and not even the vicar was inclined to answer it. Lydia, meanwhile, was eager to get her aunt away from the scene before her nerves could overcome her. She was looking very pale, and trembling dreadfully.

'Let us go home, Aunt Camilla.' She spoke gently but was insistent in pulling her along to the open gate leading to the wide lane outside the churchyard.

In a few minutes, they were at her aunt's cottage, where that good lady immediately took to her bed. For once, Lydia did not blame her. Indeed, she was much inclined to follow Camilla's example. Mrs Wardle-Penfield might not be able to discern a motive for the killing of Kate Eccles, but Lydia could. In her mind, she heard Kate's voice as it had been that afternoon at Bellefleur. Something she had remembered. Something she knew. Something which somebody had made sure she did not reveal to anyone else. Somebody had been willing to kill to keep Kate from telling what she had seen. But who was it? And would anyone ever know the truth, now that the maid was dead?

What Lydia later learned of the events which transpired that day, she got from John. He accompanied his father to Bellefleur and helped to interview the servants. They did not trouble Sir Hector. As Mrs Chalfont explained, it was useless to ask him anything. His mind was wandering, and he could certainly have nothing to say which was pertinent to the death of Kate.

The other servants were hardly more enlightening. For all the help they gave, they might as well have been laid up in bed with their master. Only Mrs Chalfont was of any assistance, and it was her evidence which John recounted to Lydia that very evening.

It was Mrs Chalfont who found the girl's body. It must have been a great shock, for John could not recall ever having seen the housekeeper so distraught. He considered her a cold, haughty woman, but she seemed genuinely distressed at what had occurred. He was almost inclined to consider her emotions rather excessive. It was, of course, a terrible tragedy, but the normally reserved housekeeper was several times on the verge of tears as she recounted what had happened that day.

'How did you come to discover the body, ma'am?' Mr Savidge asked her, himself somewhat more gentle than was customary for him.

'I – well, really, I hardly know.' The lady looked down at her hands, up at the ceiling – anywhere but at the JP or his son, seated just to his right.

'Take your time, Mrs Chalfont,' John suggested. 'Think back to what occurred just before you found Kate.'

She attempted to follow his advice, pausing for several moments to gather her thoughts and her emotions together into something coherent. She had assumed, she said, that Kate was gone to church as she usually did of a Sunday morning. She had not seen her for half an hour or more. Like the other members of the household, she neither heard nor saw anything unusual at first.

'But then,' she went on slowly, choosing her words with almost too much care, 'I glanced out of a window and saw a man. . . .'

'A man?' Mr Savidge was quick to catch this important piece of information.

'It was just for a moment.' Mrs Chalfont seemed eager to impress this point upon them. 'Just a figure in the garden. I thought . . . but really, I could not be sure. . . .'

'What did you think?' John pressed her.

'The gentleman was wearing an old-fashioned frock coat,' she explained. 'I thought it might be the Frenchman. It is the kind he wears, I believe.'

'Monsieur d'Almain?' Mr Savidge demanded.

'Yes sir.'

'Has he been to Bellefleur before?' John asked.

'Once or twice,' she nodded assent. 'It was more than a year ago, but he had some business to conduct with Sir Hector, I believe.'

'Indeed?' His father's voice was grim, John noticed.

'I could not swear that the figure I saw was Mr d'Almain,'

142

Mrs Chalfont stressed again. 'It was just out of the corner of my eye, so to speak. But it made me curious, because we certainly were not expecting any visitors.'

She went into the garden to confront the person she had seen, but there was no sign of them. They had, it seemed, disappeared. Still, she decided to look about for any further sign of the mysterious visitor. It was while she was searching that she turned a corner of the garden and almost stumbled over Kate's body lying along the path by the yew hedge.

'Such a turn it gave me,' Mrs Chalfont confessed, closing her eyes momentarily and placing a hand over her breast as if to still her beating heart. 'I hope never to see such a sight again in my life.'

'Were you aware, Mrs Chalfont,' John asked her, 'of a conversation between Kate and Miss Bramwell when she visited Bellefleur last week?'

'Conversation?' The housekeeper stared at him blankly before continuing, 'I know I sent Kate to check on the young lady, as she came over faint from the heat. I don't know what she could have had to say to her, sir.'

'It is not important.' John smiled kindly at her, and the interview was concluded.

That was all that she had to say. Only the cook supplied anything else of interest. Asked whether she had seen any strangers on the grounds at Bellefleur, she was eager to add something to the stewpot of scandal.

'Poachers, you mean?' she demanded of them. 'Aye, no doubt we've had a few of them hereabouts – probably some of that Diddlington Gang you found in the woods! And Lord knows it's been some strange goings-on in this house lately!'

'How so?' Mr Savidge enquired politely.

'Noises, sir,' she said, nodding sagely. 'Lights in rooms where nobody should be at all hours of the night, and things moved out of place – at least so the maids tell me. And the garden dug up more than once, though what anyone could be wanting with flowers and herbs and such . . . it don't make sense, sir.'

'Has Mrs Chalfont complained of anything?'

'Her?' Cook gave a snort of contempt. 'Does what she wants, and has that poor Mr Tweedy for a tame lapdog.'

Deciding that it was best not to become embroiled in domestic politics, Mr Savidge smiled and commented, 'Well, if you discover any ghosts, ma'am, you must send for me.'

'Ghosts!' Cook was highly affronted, appearing like a poor man's version of Mrs Wardle-Penfield at her most forbidding. 'I've been at Bellefleur nigh on thirty years, Mr Savidge, and there ain't no ghosts in this 'ere house. *That* I can swear to.'

'Do you know of any enemies Kate might have had?' John enquired, returning to more practical matters.

'I can't say, sir,' the old woman answered. 'She didn't even have a young man that I know of.'

That avenue seemed fruitless, so he tried another.

'And you last saw her this morning?'

'I was just preparing the meat for dinner,' she explained, 'when I looks up and sees Kate passing by, dressed for church.'

'And how long after that did Mrs Chalfont give the alarm?'

'Not more than quarter of an hour.'

'You are quite certain of that?'

'I am.'

John pondered this. It was an absurdly short span of time. Of course it did not take very long to kill. No, not long at all.

When John had finished reciting this news to Lydia, her spirits were lower than they had ever been in all her seventeen years. It would have been bad enough if her efforts had produced nothing. Instead, they had made everything infinitely worse.

'Oh John!' she almost wailed. 'What have I done?'

'It is foolish to blame yourself, Lydia,' John told her with his usual common sense.

'Had I not gone up to Bellefleur, asking questions and generally interfering in things which did not concern me, Kate would be alive today.'

'You are hardly responsible for Kate's death.' John held her by the shoulders and looked squarely into her eyes. 'It was not you who placed that cord around her neck. It was somebody whose heart has become hardened to evil – which yours clearly has not.'

'But whatever it was she remembered that day,' Lydia persisted, 'that was what led to her death. Whoever killed her knew that she was going to speak with me after church and they made very sure that she never got there.'

'Even if that is true, you are not the one at fault.'

'But it was my going there which led to all this.'

He apparently realized that it was useless to argue with her in her present emotional state, and so he wisely turned the conversation in another direction. This was to prove almost equally unhappy, however.

'At least,' he said, 'this has proven that your suspicions were correct.'

'My suspicions?'

'Obviously, someone at Bellefleur is a killer, and that person was almost certainly responsible for the death of Mr Cole.'

'And now,' she added, her head bent and held in her two hands, as though weighed down by an intolerable burden, 'now everyone will believe that Monsieur d'Almain is the murderer.'

'You can hardly blame yourself for *that* as well,' John groaned, becoming impatient with her self-imposed martyrdom. 'If you want to blame anyone, blame Mrs Chalfont.'

'She only told you what she saw.'

'Or thought she saw,' John corrected. 'She merely said that it *might* have been d'Almain, after all.'

'Which is all that is needed to confirm what has been said in the village for weeks!'

'I wonder if she is aware of the village gossip?'

'She must know!' Lydia protested. 'Unless she is deaf. I'm sure the servants at Bellefleur have tongues, and they must be repeating all that goes on in Diddlington.'

'Well, at least this must clear Sir Hector of suspicion, in your mind,' John said. 'He is clearly in no condition to commit such a crime.'

'He could have easily paid someone else to do it for him,' Lydia pointed out.

'True.' He frowned. 'But there is more to this than meets the eye.'

'I wish I had never gotten mixed up in it,' she cried with genuine sincerity.

'I did warn you of the danger,' he answered, not without a certain grim satisfaction.

'To me!' she reminded him. 'I was willing to take the risk. But how could I imagine that it could lead to someone else's death?'

'For my part,' John said practically, 'I am glad that, if someone had to perish, it was Kate Eccles and not you.'

'How heartless!' Lydia was shocked at this ruthless point of view.

'Well, I was not intending to marry *her*.'

He stood up and took a brief turn about the room. Lydia wished that she could find fault with this argument, but it was perfectly reasonable.

'What do you think,' she asked instead, 'will happen to Monsieur d'Almain?'

'My father will have him in for questioning,' he answered promptly. 'Well, he must. I only hope that he can prove that he was elsewhere this morning between the hours when Kate was last seen alive and the time Mrs Chalfont found her.'

'And if he cannot?'

'I'm afraid my father will have little choice but to arrest him.'

'You do not really think that he. . . ?' her voice trailed off, afraid to even voice the question.

'I don't know,' John said, not pretending that he didn't understand what she was suggesting. 'Until today, I would have sworn it to be impossible and I still find it hard to establish a connection between d'Almain and anyone at Bellefleur. But Kate is dead. I must wait until I hear from the man himself.'

'Will you tell me what you discover?'

'I have told you more than I should have already.' He came to stand beside her and put his arm around her shoulders in a gesture partly tender and partly bracing. 'But if anyone deserves to know, it is you, and I know I can trust you completely.'

With that, he was gone. Now she had to wait, and to hope that nothing worse might happen.

CHAPTER SEVENTEEN

SUSPICION UNLIMITED

John might be circumspect in his speech, but either his father or the housekeeper was not so cautious. By the next day, the news had somehow escaped that Mrs Chalfont had seen the French gentleman in the garden just before the poor maid was murdered. Lydia had certainly never mentioned the matter to anyone. Her tongue was not so loose, for one thing and, for another, she was really afraid to think of what the effect might be upon her aunt.

Lydia herself heard it from none other than the Misses Digweed, whom she happened to see when she looked through the front window. They were passing by on their way into Diddlington to harass the butcher for some mutton, and could not stay, but they beckoned her outside for a moment and were quick to inform her of the latest *on dit*.

'He was in the shrubbery,' said the eldest.

'The rose garden,' her sister corrected.

'With a knife.'

'A rope.'

'Such a nice gentleman.'

'Choking the life out of her.'

'So polite.'

'Menacing, I'd call him.'

'Bound to be arrested.'

'Bound to be.'

On this last point, for once they were both in agreement. By the time they finished speaking, Lydia's head was aching. They were eager to be gone, but not as eager as she was to see the backs of them. How was she to keep this from her aunt?

As it turned out, Aunt Camilla was so overset by the news from the previous day that she did not leave her bed. It was an unexpected mercy that she was closeted in her bedchamber and so heard nothing of what was happening in the world outside. When she did manage to ask her niece if there was any news, Lydia replied that it was too soon yet to know just what had happened. She urged her aunt to put the matter from her mind for the moment, and told the maid not to breathe a word of anything she might hear.

In the meantime, she sent round a note to the Golden Cockerel, begging John to please see her as soon as possible. All day long she stayed indoors, attending to her aunt and fretting herself into a state of near exhaustion. Never had she been so weary; never had the future looked so dismal.

After the most interminable day she had ever endured, at half past eight that evening there was a knock at the front door. Lydia flew to answer it, almost falling upon John's chest when he entered.

'What news?' she said breathlessly, not even bothering to greet him properly.

He shook his head slowly.

'It is not good.'

Lydia had expected as much. Indeed, she was growing so accustomed to bad news that she felt nothing could surprise her anymore. Nevertheless, it could not but add to her burden.

'What has happened?' she asked with the calm born of resignation rather than hope.

'My father brought Monsieur d'Almain in to be questioned.'

'I suppose he could not account for his movements yesterday morning?'

'He was walking – alone – in the vicinity of Bellefleur.'

Lydia closed her eyes. 'How could he have been so foolish?'

'To confess something so damning?'

'To be so absurdly honest, when the situation clearly called for a little dissimulation!'

John smiled at her.

'Perhaps he is not such an accomplished liar,' he suggested ironically, 'and feared that the truth might well come out later.'

'He has done his best to make himself appear guilty.'

'Is that because he is clever, honest, or. . . ?'

'Or merely stupid,' she finished for him.

'He admitted that he had visited Bellefleur on several occasions in the past,' John informed her, settling himself comfortably in a chair across from her. 'Apparently, Sir Hector had privately commissioned him to design a presentation box as a gift for his valet, in honour of his years of devoted service.'

'Does Mr Tweedy have such a box?' she asked.

John nodded. 'We have already confirmed that he received such a box last Christmas.'

'Then we know that d'Almain was telling the truth.'

'In that instance,' John assented.

'You do not really believe him capable of murder?'

'Most of us are capable of murder,' he answered, 'given the proper circumstances.'

'I simply cannot imagine him strangling poor Kate,' Lydia insisted.

'Nor can I. But someone did. Someone she knew.'

This captured her attention at once, and her eyes narrowed as she contemplated her betrothed.

'How can you be sure that she knew her killer?'

'If she was killed where her body was found,' John explained, 'it seems improbable that she was confronted by a stranger.'

'How so?'

He leaned back in his chair, tapping his fingers on the arm while he collected his thoughts before speaking. He said that, after examining the body and the area surrounding it more closely, he could perceive no signs of a struggle. Nor was there any place nearby where someone could hide from view. The hedge was against a wall which blocked the view from the house, but there was no space amongst the bushes for someone to hide: they were packed too closely together.

'In spite of what Mrs Chalfont and the other servants might think,' he concluded, 'Kate could not have been taken by surprise.'

'You mean that she was simply speaking to someone in the garden, and she. . . .'

'She turned around,' John finished her thought, 'and whoever was there with her, quickly slipped the cord about her neck and tightened it.'

'How horrible!' Lydia caught her lips between her teeth and stared unseeingly at the floor.

'But very simple.'

'And then the killer just slipped away unseen.' Lydia looked up at him again.

'Or returned to the house as though nothing had happened.'

'So you *do* suspect someone at Bellefleur!'

'I suspect *everyone* at Bellefleur,' he said with a smile.

'Except Sir Hector,' she quizzed him.

'Tell me,' he asked, ignoring her last remark, 'who overheard Kate's remark to you that afternoon?'

'Mr Tweedy did,' she said promptly. 'He came up behind her as she stood at the door, talking to me.'

'And nobody else was about?'

'Nobody,' she asserted confidently.

'I think I had better have a word with Mr Tweedy

tomorrow,' John said, rising from his seat.

'Please be careful, John,' she urged him.

He put his arm around her as she came up beside him.

'How long has it been since I kissed you, Lydia?'

'Much too long,' she said, pouting.

He promptly remedied the situation. Then, after a considerable amount of time had passed, he stepped back and straightened his neck cloth.

'I had best leave before I forget that we are not yet married!'

'Do you think we shall ever be?' she asked doubtfully.

'What kind of talk is this?' he demanded.

'Your father is right, John,' she said seriously. 'You can do much better for yourself than to marry me. I seem to do nothing but cause trouble.'

'You certainly do not sit at home stitching samplers,' he agreed with a grin. 'But that's not the sort of wife I'm hanging out for, love.'

'I'm not very pretty,' she said, pressing home her point.

'You're not a beauty,' he agreed, not being one to pay empty compliments. 'But I'm no Adonis either. I like your face. It suits me.'

'I think I should cry off.' She sighed, not at all offended by his honesty. 'After all, we do not yet know what my father will say.'

'It does not matter what he says,' John replied with cheerful ruthlessness. 'Unless you want to be branded a fast female and a jilt, you must marry me.'

'I think,' she said a little wistfully, 'that it might be rather pleasant to be considered a fast female.'

'Not at all the thing,' he corrected her. 'You wouldn't like it at all.'

'You may be right.'

'Of course I am.'

CHAPTER EIGHTEEN

THE COURSE OF TRUE LOVE

The following day, Aunt Camilla felt well enough to come downstairs and have some toast and a little weak tea. She still did not feel strong enough to venture out of doors, and Lydia was beginning to think that the evil moment might be put off indefinitely – but it was not to be.

The two women had not been downstairs together for more than a quarter of an hour before they were forced to receive a visitor: Mrs Wardle-Penfield. She protruded into the room rather like the bow of a ship jutting out over a dock. In this case, it would have been a naval vessel engaged in battle, for her words fell like cannon balls into the placid waters of her aunt's sitting-room, throwing up a splash and unsettling everyone.

It did not take her long to fire the first shot, proclaiming that Monsieur d'Almain had been questioned by Mr Savidge the previous day and had practically confessed to murdering poor Kate Eccles! Shameless, she called it: posi-

tively shameless. To be killing people when his good neighbours were all at their prayers! Those monstrous French
... good for nothing but revolution and rebellion. Well, he
should have a taste of English justice now. It was a pity,
though, that the English did not at least allow the use of
the guillotine.

To Lydia's surprise, her aunt sat through this swelling
diatribe in complete silence and apparently in full
command of her faculties. So stiff and straight she was that
Lydia presently began to wonder if she had not died and
her body stiffened with *rigor mortis*.

At length Mrs Wardle-Penfield concluded her speech and
relieved them of her presence, saying that she must be off
to the inn to find out whether or not the Frenchman had
yet been arrested.

After seeing her to the door, Lydia returned to the room
to find Camilla gone. She dashed up the stairs to her aunt's
bedchamber. The door was open, and her aunt was plainly
visible as she struggled to put on a bottle green spencer
and a neat round bonnet.

'Where are you going, aunt?' Lydia asked in some
consternation. Never had she seen the older woman so
active and vigorous.

'I must go to him, Lydia,' Camilla stated, her voice strong
and sure, though her hands trembled as she tied the
ribbons under her chin in a lop-sided bow. 'He is my love,
my life! He needs me, and I shall not fail him.'

Lydia blinked. She could only be referring to Monsieur
d'Almain.

'I shall go with you,' she said.

'Do as you please.'

Within minutes they were walking down the high street on their way to the Frenchman's lodgings. Lydia almost had to run to keep pace with her relative, who was progressing much faster than usual. She passed by several of her acquaintance without even acknowledging their presence, and it was left to Lydia to attempt a polite bow as they flitted away. They were attracting considerable attention, for it was clear even to the most disinterested observer that this was no mere afternoon stroll.

At last they reached the door of the gentleman's humble house, and Aunt Camilla knocked loudly. It was a matter only of seconds before the occupant opened it and stared at them both with a look of astonishment on his handsome countenance.

'Miss Denton . . . Miss Bramwell,' d'Almain began formally, but his speech was forestalled.

'I came as soon as I heard,' Aunt Camilla began, going forward impetuously and leaving her niece to close the door behind them. 'Oh Monsieur d'Almain, tell me that it is not so!'

'I assure you, ma'am, that I am innocent of any misdeed with which they seek to charge me.'

'Oh sir,' Camilla choked out the words, 'never could I believe any such wicked slander against you! But if anything were to happen to you—'

Here she put them both completely out of countenance by succumbing to a sudden bout of weeping which prohibited further speech. Lydia would have rushed forward to

158

help her, but she perceived at once that d'Almain already had the situation – along with her aunt – firmly in hand.

'Oh, my dearest love,' he said most improperly, clasping her in his manly arms, 'I would have done anything to spare you this pain and distress.'

'I could not bear it,' Camilla sobbed into his chest, 'if I should lose you.'

'*Mon ange*,' he cried, 'how I have dreamed of holding you in my arms! But not like this.'

Lydia felt as if she were at a stage play. Louisa could not witness a more tender love scene at Drury Lane! She found a convenient chair in a corner of the room and settled back to enjoy the spectacle before her.

'Am I truly your dearest love, Monsieur?' Camilla whispered, looking up at him through tear-studded lashes. 'Do you care for me, sir?'

'You are more to me than all the jewels in all the crowns of Europe!' he said. 'You are my life, my soul!'

'Oh, Monsieur d'Almain!' her aunt sighed appropriately, and her lips parted for the expected kiss. However, in this she was disappointed.

With a cry of anguish, the gentleman thrust her unceremoniously away from him.

'What a worm am I!' he said. 'How can I declare my love at such a moment? How can I offer for you when such a cloud hangs over my head?'

'If you love me, nothing else matters.'

'*If* I love you!' He seemed somewhat offended at the suggestion that he might not. 'From the first moment I saw you, you are all I have dreamed of, all I have longed for.

Mon coeur, mon amour!'

With the culmination of this effluvia of passion, he finally screwed up the courage – or decided that the timing was perfect – to kiss her. It was a long, deep, kiss which might have lasted even longer had not Camilla chosen that moment to swoon quietly away.

With a cry of anguish, Monsieur d'Almain lifted her in his arms and placed her gently on a shabby sofa near the front window. Lydia, somewhat annoyed with her aunt for ending such an interesting moment of high drama, plucked the hartshorn from Camilla's reticule. In a moment, the lady had revived enough to continue her discussion with the gentleman who could at last be officially designated as her lover.

'*Voici!'* he cried, kneeling beside her makeshift bed. 'You are better, *n'est-ce pas?'*

His beloved would doubtless have reassured him on this point, but she was prevented by a loud banging upon the door of the humble cot.

'Who can that be?' Lydia wondered aloud.

'Henri d'Almain,' a harsh voice penetrated clearly through the thick wood, 'we demand that you open to us at once!'

Lydia recognized the voice: it was Thomas Savidge. The others knew it also.

'No!' Aunt Camilla cried hysterically, clutching at Monsieur d'Almain's hand as he would have risen to honour Mr Savidge's request. 'They will take you away from me, Henri! They will kill you.'

'It is useless to resist,' the Frenchman replied with noble

resignation. He gently removed her hand and turned to admit his persecutors, while Camilla fainted away for the second time.

It had been a most exhilarating day, Lydia reflected later that evening after coming down from Aunt Camilla's bedchamber. That poor lady was, quite naturally, prostrate upon her bed and only managed to sleep after being administered a strong dose of tea and a sedative draught.

'I do not know what to do, John,' she admitted when she joined him in the parlour below.

'How is she?' he asked, referring to her aunt.

'As well as may be expected, given her nature and the present circumstances.'

'I understand that he practically proposed to her?' John enquired.

'He did indeed.'

'Damnfool thing to do.'

'So I thought.' She nodded. 'But he is clearly as romantic as she is. They should deal famously together.'

'Let us hope that the wedding ceremony is not performed beneath a hangman's noose,' John commented drily.

'Oh no!' Lydia shook her head decisively. 'We cannot allow that.'

'The only way to prevent it, I'm afraid, is to find the real killer.'

'But how?'

'I think I had better pay another visit to Bellefleur,' he said soberly. 'Although I wish I knew what I was looking for.'

They both sat silent for several minutes, each engrossed in their separate attempts to review what they had learned so far, to try and make some sense of it all. It was in this silence that they suddenly heard the unmistakable sound of an approaching carriage. At first they paid little heed to it. They were close enough to the high street that this was not an unusual noise. But their attention was truly captured when the sounds seemed to halt directly outside. There were voices raised, followed by the sound of someone at the front door.

'Who can that be?' Lydia asked for the second time that day. There was only one way to discover the truth.

She hurried to the door, John in her wake, and cautiously opened it. After all, the way things stood now, one never could tell what one might find.

The gentleman who stood outside, looking somewhat tired and harassed, was a stranger to John and certainly the last person Lydia had ever expected to see.

'Papa!' she cried, feeling an illogical sense not merely of happiness but also of immediate optimism. Everything would be all right now that her father was here.

'It seems,' Mr Bramwell declared, returning his daughter's embrace, 'that you have been having a much more interesting time here in the country than we have in London.'

CHAPTER NINETEEN

FRESH REVELATIONS

Nothing could have been better timed than Mr Bramwell's unexpected visit. It was as good as a tonic. Lydia's flagging spirits revived at once. Her aunt, immediately informed of his arrival, managed to rouse herself from her former stupor to come downstairs. Perhaps only John greeted him with emotions which were not entirely positive in nature. He was well aware that the older man would be judging the suitability of Master John Savidge as a future son-in-law.

Amidst the noise of introductions and assorted exclamations, Lydia managed to introduce the two men. They exchanged a polite handshake while surreptitiously inspecting each other. What either of them concluded at this point was a matter of conjecture, but it was some consolation to note that neither displayed any notable distaste. In appearance, at least, they both seemed satisfied.

There was quite a contrast between them, Lydia thought

to herself. Her father was of middling height, slender but strong, with thinning brown hair, but always very neat and almost dandified in appearance. John, of course, was a giant of a man who dressed with a carelessness which did not quite disguise the excellent cut of his attire.

They settled themselves in the same drawing-room which inevitably hosted any gathering in Camilla Denton's cottage. Before they could proceed to any topics of real importance, the usual preliminary trivialities must be got through.

'How did you come here, Papa?' Lydia could not refrain from asking.

'A hired chaise,' Mr Bramwell replied with a slight smile.

'How ruinously expensive!' Aunt Camilla exclaimed, almost forgetting her broken heart and shattered nerves in the contemplation of so rash an action.

'A trifle extravagant, perhaps,' he conceded, 'but I felt that the occasion warranted the expense.'

'I would be happy,' John interjected awkwardly but sincerely, 'to defray the cost. . . .'

'Nonsense, Mr Savidge.' The older man could not resist a twinkle. 'I could not so importune one who is soon to become a son to me.'

'If you will give us your blessing, sir,' John replied less stiffly, beginning to comprehend Mr Bramwell and immediately warming to him.

'I do not know that I dare object.'

'Do be serious, Papa,' his daughter admonished him.

'I shall try,' he answered doubtfully.

'All here is chaos and disorder!' Camilla warned him.

'Such goings-on as were never seen in Diddlington, brother. I do not know that I shall ever recover from it.'

'Murder and smuggling in the woods . . .' Mr Bramwell looked around on them all, his brows raised. 'What more could one wish for, indeed?'

'It has certainly not been dull,' Lydia agreed.

'And now your betrothal, my dear,' he added, bestowing a smile upon her.

'Nay, sir,' she corrected him, glancing at her aunt. 'Not one but two betrothals!'

'How is this?' He laughed outright at this. 'Perhaps I never explained to you that you cannot marry two gentlemen at once. A foolish law, I warrant you, but there it is.'

'Not I, but my aunt. She is to marry a felon who is even now in the Diddlington gaol.'

'My dear Camilla,' Mr Bramwell leaned over to take the hand of his sister-in-law, 'I felicitate you! A felon, you say? It quite eclipses Lydia's achievement.'

'Oh!' Camilla buried her face in her handkerchief, the tears beginning to flow once more. 'How can you jest about something so terrible?'

'I fear the Bramwells are not noted for their sensibility, ma'am,' he confessed charmingly. 'Is the gentleman in question one of the smugglers so lately apprehended?'

'Oh no, sir.' John was eager to disabuse him of this mistaken conjecture. 'He is charged with murder.'

'The murder of the gentleman who shared the stage with my daughter?'

'No, no,' Lydia reassured him on this point. 'One of the

servants at Bellefleur was strangled on Sunday morning.'

'It is a wicked lie!' Camilla cried out passionately. 'Henri would never even imagine something so vile. I know he would not.'

'We are all agreed that Monsieur d'Almain is innocent of the crime,' John seconded her championship of the absent Frenchman.

'I am glad to hear it.' Mr Bramwell folded his arms as he regarded them with mock solemnity. 'A thief one might welcome into the family fold. A thief, after all, may have his uses if one is in straitened circumstances. But a murderer . . . one does not relish the connection, particularly if one is spending the night under his roof. One must feel a certain . . . restraint, as it were.'

'You are a rare one, sir,' John said appreciatively.

'We are going to find the real murderer,' Lydia contributed blithely, 'so that we can clear Monsieur d'Almain and he can marry Aunt Camilla.'

'A laudable ambition. I suppose it will not be difficult to discover the identity of the murderer?'

'No trouble at all, I assure you,' John answered, with a wry look at his intended.

'If you mean to quiz me, John,' she shot back at him, 'I warn you that I refuse to be baited!'

'Your daughter, sir,' John directed his next remark to the other gentleman, 'is never at a loss for a scheme of some kind.'

'It seems,' Mr Bramwell commented in return, 'that Diddlington is never at a loss to supply a murder for the employment of one of her schemes. It would appear to be all the rage, in fact. A Shakespeare tragedy could not supply such a surfeit of corpses.'

'It is like a plague!' Aunt Camilla complained, adding in dire tones, 'Many have taken to locking their doors.'

'Surely there is no need for such drastic measures,' her brother-in-law objected. 'Next you will be seeking help from Bow Street!'

'As exciting as that would be, I think we need not send for the Runners yet,' John said, 'with Lydia in hot pursuit of the villains.'

'Stuff!' Lydia objected crossly. 'You know that you are as eager as I am to learn the truth.'

'But not so intrepid,' he said with a bow.

'Or so foolhardy,' Camilla snapped, probably more accurately than she knew.

'Well, compared to all this,' Mr Bramwell sighed, looking absurdly crestfallen, 'my news from town will seem frightfully tame.'

'What news?' Lydia demanded instantly.

'Is it my sister?' Camilla clutched at her chest, always prepared to hear the worst.

'Is it Louisa?'

Mr Bramwell leaned back in his chair, pausing for an interminable period which could not have been less than five seconds. He was determined to produce the most dramatic effect from his performance.

'Mrs Bramwell is in excellent health,' he said at last, 'so you may be easy on that head, Camilla. She is a little concerned that her daughter and sister reside in a village whose chief business seems to be that of murdering its inhabitants and she has discovered that she is far from partial to young men named "Savidge". Aside from this, however, she has never been better.'

'I shall not easily win the lady's favour, it seems,' John ruminated aloud.

'Never fear,' Lydia's father comforted him. 'You need only win *my* favour, lad. In fact, my wife charged me particularly to determine whether you are worthy of our daughter.'

'And is your initial impression favourable?'

'Well . . .' Mr Bramwell stroked his chin with slow deliberation. 'It is best not to be too hasty in one's judgments.'

'I can tell that Papa likes you, John,' Lydia explained unnecessarily. Then, turning to her father, she added, 'You still have not told us anything that is happening in London, sir.'

'It seems,' the older man informed them, 'that I may soon have both daughters married.'

'No!' Lydia cried, truly astonished.

'Is Louisa also betrothed, then?' Camilla was equally amazed, and quite impressed.

'It has not progressed as far as that.' Mr Bramwell held up a cautionary finger, indicating that they should not celebrate precipitately. 'But she certainly has a suitor who, your mama assures me, has developed a decided *tendre* for her. And, if that were not enough, he is a member of the peerage.'

There was an appreciative gasp from the female members of his small audience. John's eyes widened, but he gave no other indication of his surprise.

'Never tell me,' Lydia exclaimed, 'that Louisa has got herself a Duke after all!'

'That *would* be a prize catch!' Mr Bramwell chuckled, enjoying himself hugely. 'No, I fear your sister will be forced to settle for a mere baronet.'

'How shabby.' Lydia was almost disappointed for her sister. Indeed, she had never felt less spiteful towards her.

'Considering what Lydia has told me of Louisa's behaviour,' Camilla said frankly, 'I find it hard to believe that she has managed to attach anyone at all.'

'You could not be more surprised than Mrs Bramwell and I,' her brother-in-law confessed. 'Even Louisa, I believe, found it difficult to credit her good fortune – if such it can be called. She certainly means to have the gentleman, and declares that she would rather die than to return home unmarried.'

'That sounds like Louisa,' Lydia nodded her head emphatically. 'But tell us, Papa, who is he? And how did this come about?'

It seemed that soon after the affair of the pink gown, Louisa had managed to find a secluded corner where she could indulge a fit of mild hysterics in unmolested solitude. However, her sniffling had attracted the attention of one solitary gentleman, Sir Reginald Pevensey, who offered a handkerchief and managed to talk her out of her megrims. He had called at their lodgings the next day to ensure that Miss Bramwell was not laid low by her affliction. Assured that she was much recovered, he offered to take her walking in Green Park. Naturally, there was no question of declining such a gracious invitation.

For the past ten days, his attentions had been so marked that Mrs Bramwell and her daughter lived in hourly expectation of receiving an offer. Indeed, Mr Bramwell continued, he had been given express instructions not to remain any longer in Diddlington than was strictly necessary; for he must be present in London should the blessed event occur. His consent, of course, was a foregone conclusion. How could it be otherwise?

'What is he like, sir?' Lydia asked when her parent paused in his fascinating narrative. 'He cannot be very sensible, I think, or he would not want to marry Louisa.'

'His intellect may not be superior.' Mr Bramwell was willing to concede this point. 'But his manners are polished and his estate is large. Louisa will have all the pin-money she could desire, and more than enough servants to bully. I could wish that he were a little younger. . . .'

'How old is he?' Camilla asked at once.

'He will never see fifty again, unless he looks a considerable distance behind him.'

Once more there was an incoherent exclamation from the ladies, while John closed his lips determinedly.

'Papa!' Lydia squealed. 'He is older than you are!'

'Only by seven or eight years, my dear.'

'She cannot be in love with him,' Aunt Camilla declared. 'It is not possible.'

'Louisa is very much in love . . . with herself!' Lydia said with less than charity. 'But it is a far cry from the handsome prince she boasted she would get.'

'A well-heeled widower is not a match to be ignored,' Mr Bramwell answered practically, 'especially when one's own fortune is . . . negligible.'

'Invisible, you mean,' Lydia said bluntly. 'I suppose, as things stand, she has little choice in the matter. But do you think she will be happy?'

'She would certainly not be happy living the rest of her life as an impoverished spinster,' Aunt Camilla assured them fervently, and with the authority of one who had actually experienced a similar fate.

'All things considered,' Mr Bramwell said, 'I think my daughter has done better for herself than she ever deserved. As for Sir Reginald, poor devil . . . well, perhaps a fool deserves to suffer the consequences of his own folly.'

Later that night, when Mr Bramwell had been comfortably installed in the one remaining bedchamber, Lydia snuggled down in her bed beneath the embroidered counterpane and considered her own situation in light of all that had happened these past weeks.

It must be a triumph for her mother, she supposed, to have both of her daughters engaged to be married at the same time! Mrs Bramwell might be somewhat doubtful about the young man her youngest child had chosen, but on the whole there could be no doubt that her cup was now about to overflow.

However, at this juncture, Lydia began to entertain doubts as to whether marrying John was the right step for her to be taking. Louisa, for all her romantic rattle, had settled for money rather than love. Aunt Camilla, on the other hand, had cast aside intellect in favour of over-whelming emotion.

Lydia could honestly say that there was nothing mercenary in her determination to wed John. His father was plump in the pocket, true enough, but she knew nothing of John's own prospects. It was neither security nor wealth that she desired.

On the other hand, judged by her aunt's standards, their marriage would not be founded on romantic passion either. She truly esteemed John. She certainly enjoyed his kisses and looked forward to whatever pleasure the marriage bed might provide. But she did not consider him to be the most handsome man on earth. Her heart skipped no beat when she beheld his face. Being in his arms was a pleasant experience, to be sure, but she felt no inclination to swoon in his presence. The mention of his name did not drive all other thoughts from her mind, and she would have to think very carefully before she could be convinced to give up all she held dear for his sake.

No. She was not in love with John. But she did love him. It was a steady, strong affection and a recognition within herself that they were much alike and would be able to build a good and happy life together. There might be no peaks of ecstasy, as Aunt Camilla would surely know with d'Almain, but there would be no valleys of despair either. They would be companions throughout life. In good times they would share a placid contentment and much laughter; in times of crisis, they would be united in facing whatever might come to them.

The question was: was that enough? After due consideration, the answer was that, for herself, it was more than enough. But what of John? Perhaps he expected more from marriage. Could she, in all conscience, deprive him of that emotional whirlwind which love provided those who enjoyed being giddy and foolish?

She was seriously contemplating breaking their engagement. Her mind told her that they were well suited, but the fashion nowadays was for men and women to wed for no other reason than that they conceived a wild attraction for one another – however ill-suited they might be, and however little prospect of lasting happiness their union could provide.

Of course, John did not seem to be a slave to fashion, but one never knew. In the end, the only thing she supposed that she could do was to speak to him about it and find out what he thought of the matter. With a brief prayer that he would be honest with her (but then, John was not one to practice deception), she turned on her side and fell asleep almost immediately.

CHAPTER TWENTY

OF LOVE AND MARRIAGE

When she awoke the next morning, Lydia soon discovered that her father had already taken himself off. His expressed destination, she was informed, was the Golden Cockerel. It was plain that his mission was to become better acquainted with John, and perhaps to speak with the young man's father as well. Although Lydia fully expected a positive outcome from the meeting, she still could feel a small twinge of apprehension as she waited quietly with Aunt Camilla, who was not a very loquacious companion, being preoccupied with her own dilemma and thoughts of her beloved which must be anything but comforting.

Positioning herself strategically beside the front window, it was a full two hours before the figure Lydia sought passed by. To be precise, it was not one but two figures which came into view as they made their way to the front door. Papa had brought John back with him.

They seemed to be on very good terms, and Lydia breathed a sigh of relief that things had gone so smoothly. Her father was as eager to accept her intended as anyone could reasonably wish.

John informed them that they were all invited to the inn that evening to dine with him and his father.

'And I understand that it will be in the nature of a celebration.' He gave a broad wink. 'It seems that someone in this room will be marking a particular milestone on the morrow.'

'Good gracious!' Lydia exclaimed. She had completely forgotten that tomorrow was her eighteenth birthday.

'How could you forget something so important?' her aunt wondered aloud.

'With so much happening,' Mr Bramwell remarked, 'it is little wonder that the poor child should be forgetful.'

'But you are a day early, sir!' Aunt Camilla admonished John.

'Unfortunately, I shall be leaving tomorrow,' Mr Bramwell explained apologetically. 'I therefore thought it best to commemorate the occasion tonight. I have a small gift which you can open tomorrow, my dear.'

It was an odd gathering that evening, Lydia thought as she looked around her. They were in a small but well-appointed salon, separated from the main dining space of the inn by a heavy brocade curtain. From the other side, she could hear muted conversations and occasional bursts of laughter.

Their own party was rather subdued. How could it be

175

otherwise? Papa was spending his last night with them for some weeks; Aunt Camilla was severely blue-devilled by thoughts of her incarcerated lover, and rather cold in her attitude to her host. Lydia was feeling unusually anxious because she wanted to speak privately with John but had been granted no such opportunity as yet. John and his father were the only two who seemed perfectly at ease. The elder Savidge was more cordial since he had learned that Lydia's sister was expecting an offer from a gentleman whose name might be found in the Peerage. John was his usual placid, smiling self.

Lydia's health was toasted and she received gifts from everyone, for which she thanked them most sincerely and promised to open them the next morning. The food was excellent, for Mr Savidge always prided himself on the quality of the fare offered at his establishment.

Only when the party was about to disperse was Lydia finally able to snatch a few precious moments alone with John. Thomas Savidge had made his own carriage ready to convey them to their home, but Lydia protested that it was such a short distance that there was no need. She would much prefer to walk.

'Walk, my dear Miss Bramwell!' Mr Savidge expostulated, appalled at such a suggestion. 'Never let it be said that Thomas Savidge behaved in so shabby a fashion toward his guests.'

Part of the reason for his insistence was his burning desire to show off to all his acquaintance his latest acquisition: a smart new landau which he lost no time in having his coachman bring round for their delectation. Like a child with a new toy, he must be pointing out every detail of its manifold charms – from the folding roof, which he kept down tonight to enjoy the balmy air, to special lanterns which proclaimed its presence even on the darkest night.

'I must admit,' Mr Bramwell said, eyeing this impressive conveyance with approval, 'that I am quite fagged to death, and look forward to a short carriage ride. But for young people, no doubt an evening walk is far more pleasant.'

'If you will permit me, sir,' John said, taking Lydia's arm, 'I would be pleased to escort Miss Bramwell home. We shall not be very many minutes, I assure you.'

'Do you think it is wise?' Aunt Camilla asked, uncertain whether this exceeded the bounds of strict propriety. Besides, with a murderer loose among them, who could tell what might happen?

'My dear sister,' Mr Bramwell told her, 'when an engaged couple cannot take a stroll in the moonlight, on the village high street, things have come to a pretty pass in this country!'

So it was settled. While their elders enjoyed the comforts of their host's carriage, John and Lydia began to walk towards the cottage. It was only a few minutes after ten o'clock. The air was cool, but not unpleasantly so: just enough, in fact, to make walking a pleasant exercise rather than a chore.

The young couple watched the carriage bump along the road and out of sight before they ventured to speak to each other.

'John,' Lydia ventured at last, 'do you think that we should continue with this?'

'With what?' he asked, perhaps pardonably perplexed.

'Our engagement, I mean.'

'Do you intend to jilt me?' he queried, placid as always.

'No, no,' she said hurriedly. 'But do you think that we are doing the right thing?'

'Perhaps I should ask you why you seem to think that we are not?'

There was a brief pause while Lydia drew closer and pulled the skirt of her gown towards her in order to avoid being caught in the branch of a low bush which protruded onto the pavement beside them. When she at last spoke, the words came out in a rush, as if she had been holding them in with her breath and must release them all at once.

'It's just that I do not think that we are in love with each other, John: at least, not in the way that my aunt and Monsieur d'Almain are.'

'But we are not your aunt and d'Almain,' he pointed out. 'Our natures are not the same, and neither are our feelings.'

'Tell me honestly, John,' she begged. 'Do you think of nothing else but me, day and night?'

'Of course not!' he objected strongly. 'You are often in my thoughts, to be sure, but I have many things to think about, particularly just now. What with saving d'Almain and trying to keep my father in check. . . .'

'Just so.' But she was not finished with him yet. 'If we marry,' she continued with determination, 'and I were to perish in childbirth or something, would you put a bullet through your brains?'

'Certainly not.' He stopped and looked down at her with

a frown. 'What has put all this nonsense into your head?'

'It is merely that all the heroes in romantic novels do such things. Their love is everything in the world to them. Nothing else matters.'

John snorted contemptuously. 'That is all very well in books,' he informed her, 'but life is quite different. One would have to be decidedly touched in the upper works to do anything so silly.'

'And if I *were* to die . . .' she continued doggedly.

'Whyever should you?' he demanded. 'You are young and perfectly healthy.'

'Yes, but if I should, would you marry again?'

'Very likely,' he said. 'Particularly if we had children, and if I were not so old as to be content with no more than a lapdog for company.'

'Do you think,' she persevered, coming to the heart of the matter, 'that there is only one person – one love – for each person on earth?'

'Most unlikely, I should say,' he stated flatly. 'Frankly, I would have thought you would have more sense than this, Lydia.'

'Oh, I do!' she cried. 'I was merely wondering if you might not.'

Having resumed their perambulation, they were now within sight of Aunt Camilla's cottage. However, John stopped her once more, and turned her about to face him.

'Look here, Lydia,' he said. 'I have every intention – and indeed every desire – to marry you. But if you do not wish to marry me, I will not force you to do so.'

'Of course I wish to marry you, John!' she cried, feeling

179

as if a great weight had been lifted from her shoulders.

'Then we may consider the matter as settled.'

They walked on several more paces, and were at the front of the cottage before Lydia wondered aloud, 'Do you think that Aunt Camilla and Monsieur d'Almain will find happiness together?'

'I think,' John said, after considering the question for several moments, 'that neither one of them is ever truly happy unless they are *un*happy.'

'They are perfectly matched, then,' she said cheerfully.

'Unquestionably.'

John bent his head and gave her a most encouraging kiss. She heard no angels singing, nor did her heart leap like the fallow deer, but it was most enjoyable and she was rather annoyed when it ended.

'We must,' he told her, with a complete change of subject, 'see what we can do about clearing d'Almain of this crime.'

'It is absolutely imperative,' she agreed.

'I will return tomorrow to see your father off.' John escorted her the last few paces to the front door. 'We will make our plans then.'

CHAPTER TWENTY-ONE

THE SCENT OF MURDER

Lydia was more than pleased with the gifts which she received on her birthday. Papa had purchased a richly plumed bonnet which he assured her was all the crack in town. Aunt Camilla presented her with delicately embroidered handkerchiefs – an absolute necessity for young ladies. John's gift was an unusual cross suspended on a slender golden chain. It was, he explained, carved from a kind of jade found not in the Orient but from the equally distant shores of South America. It was not merely lovely to behold, but had the added attraction of the exotic.

Under other circumstances, it might well have been a perfect birthday. However, there was still the danger facing Monsieur d'Almain, which oppressed her aunt's spirits so dreadfully and was a constant thorn in Lydia's own side since she could not at present see any way to clear his name. In addition, Mr Bramwell's departure took away a significant source of happiness and some measure of hope. She had convinced herself that her father would be able to assist her in her efforts to find the truth about the recent crimes in Diddlington, but he had no answer to the riddles which still perplexed her.

'Can you not stay one more day?' she begged, clutching his coat sleeve even while the hired conveyance waited outside in the high street.

'I'm afraid that it is impossible, my dear.' Mr Bramwell sighed, and it was clear that he quit them with no enthusiasm. He smiled warmly at her, and then turned his gaze upon John. 'But I know that I leave you in good hands here, and I am certain that your French friend will have cause to thank you at last.'

'I hope that I shall be seeing you again soon, sir,' his future son-in-law said, shaking his hand.

'I shall doubtless be permitted to return to you once my eldest child has managed to capture her titled gudgeon.'

'Pray, give mama and Louisa my love!' Lydia cried, belatedly remembering her duty. 'I trust that I shall soon be hearing glad tidings from my sister.'

'You may hear that she is to be married,' papa answered drily. 'Whether such tidings are glad or gloomy, it is not for me to say.'

Lydia laughed. 'At least Louisa will achieve her ambition to wed a title.'

'And an *ancient* title it is too,' Mr Bramwell said with a wicked reference to the gentleman's advanced years. 'Not the handsome young buck she once imagined, I fear.'

'A baronet,' John reminded him, 'is still a baronet at any age.'

'True,' Mr Bramwell admitted. 'And she would certainly be foolish to refuse him, should he offer his heart and hand.'

'Never mind,' Lydia added, 'that the hand of a man of sixty is not so strong or so smooth as a man of twenty.'

'If his flesh be withered, it is no great matter – so long as his pockets are plump!'

Lydia turned to John, expecting him to join in their inappropriate merriment, but was surprised to see a look of utter amazement upon his usually smiling countenance. He was not smiling now, but looked from father to daughter as if he beheld them anew.

'I must be going,' Mr Bramwell announced, having put off the evil moment for as long as possible.

'Goodbye, Papa.'

Amid the bustle naturally attending any departure, Lydia momentarily forgot the strange reaction of her fiancé, and was busy in hugging her father and dabbing a spot of moisture from her cheek with Aunt Camilla's gift. Only when the carriage had disappeared around the corner did her attention return to John. The startled look was gone, she was glad to see, but its substitute was equally interesting. John now looked more grave than she had ever seen him.

'What is it, John?' she could not help but ask him.

'Lydia,' he intoned with the solemnity of a priest administering the last rites, 'we must speak.'

This had a most inauspicious ring to it, but she nodded

quietly and led him back into the house. They had been standing on the grass verge beside the street, but now made their way back into her aunt's house. Camilla herself had already fled indoors, overcome as always by the strain of parting from anyone for whom she felt even the mildest affection.

'Tell me again,' John insisted as soon as they had seated themselves in the parlour, 'just what Kate said to you that day at Bellefleur.'

'I am sure I have told you more than once,' she replied, not annoyed but curious as to why he should desire to hear it again.

'Bear with me a moment,' he pleaded.

She began to recount their conversation, as far as her memory served, and he interrupted her again, to ask what were her very last words.

'She said, "It wasn't his hands, miss",' Lydia answered confidently.

'How did she say the words?'

'As though she were surprised about something.'

'No, no,' he almost growled in his intensity. 'How did she say them? Did she say, "It wasn't *his* hands, miss?" Or did she say, "It wasn't his *hands*, miss?" '

'Does it matter?' Lydia was mystified.

John ignored the question, asking instead, 'Of whom was she speaking?'

'I really cannot be sure.'

'Think, Lydia!' he cried. 'Had she not been telling you something just before that?'

Lydia closed her eyes, summoning to mind all that had

happened that day at Bellefleur. The little maid had been eager to tell her anything that she knew, although it had not seemed to be much at the time.

'She had been telling me how she went into Sir Hector's room one day, quite unexpectedly, when she heard something fall.'

'And what happened when she went in?'

'The room was very dark, being lit by just one candle.' Lydia compressed her lips in an effort of concentration. 'Sir Hector reached over and snuffed out the candle at once, and flung some very – colourful – words at her.'

John shot up out of his chair, slapping his hand against his forehead. He began to pace about the room like one distracted, while Lydia stared up at him in a kind of wonder.

'My God!' he cried. 'What a fool I've been.'

'Whatever is the matter, John?'

John halted in his stride, standing directly over her and looking down at her with a strange mixture of triumph and sadness.

'I know who killed her, Lydia,' he said with quiet confidence.

For a few seconds Lydia was quite deprived of speech. Her mouth indeed opened, but no sound emerged from her parted lips. She did not doubt John, but it was such a sudden and unexpected development.

'How can you know?' she demanded when she at last recovered herself.

'Do you not see?' He grasped her two hands in his and

185

pulled her up to face him. 'It was the hands.'

'The hands?' Lydia was more puzzled than ever.

'Yes. I am a simpleton not to have seen it before.' He squeezed her hands painfully in his own large fingers, before continuing more slowly, 'When Kate entered that room, she saw a hand reach across to the candle. She saw it for only a moment before the room was plunged into complete darkness. It was not until she spoke to you that day that she realized the hand she saw did not belong to Sir Hector. *It wasn't his hand.*'

Lydia stared at him, allowing his words to slowly but strongly pry open the door of her mind. She understood something of what he was saying, but still did not grasp the entire meaning.

'You do not mean to say,' she gasped out, 'that Sir Hector had a woman in his bed! At his age!'

To her consternation, John flung back his head and burst into a peal of laughter. Indeed, he was so full of mirth that he quite forgot his manners, dropping back into his chair, so convulsed that he was even forced to wipe a tear or two from his eyes.

'I do not find it at all amusing,' she scolded him, not at all inclined to share his emotions.

'What is going on here?' her aunt's voice, speaking from the open doorway, distracted them both for a moment.

'John is telling me that Sir Hector was keeping a mistress at Bellefleur,' Lydia informed her.

'Impossible!' Even Camilla found this camel too large to swallow. 'Next you will be saying that Kate was his natural daughter.'

'I fear that you have misunderstood me, my love,' John corrected Lydia, having managed to gain control of his emotions.

'You mean to say,' his love demanded, 'that he had a *man* in his bed with him?'

'This grows more scandalous by the minute!' Camilla gasped, horrified.

'Calm yourselves, both of you.'

For the benefit of the older woman, he explained what he had been discussing with Lydia. Camilla, however, was no more enlightened than her niece, so John kindly undertook to explain himself more clearly.

'There was,' he said, 'only one person in the bed when Kate walked in, and that person was not Sir Hector.'

'Oh!' the two women exclaimed together.

'Sir Hector,' John continued more gravely, 'has not, I fear, been in that bed for some time – and never will again, if I am correct in my suspicions.'

'But who—?' Lydia began.

'I will say no more on that head now,' John stopped her impetuous words. 'After all, it is possible that I am mistaken – though I do not think it.'

'What are you going to do about it?' she asked.

'We are going back to Bellefleur,' he announced.

'All of us?' Aunt Camilla could not help but be surprised.

'Yes.' He nodded decisively. 'We are all involved in this, in some manner. It is only fitting that we should all be present.'

'When do we go?'

'Now. There is no time to lose.' John turned to Aunt

Camilla. 'I want you to go to Mrs Wardle-Penfield, ma'am. We will need her carriage.'

'I do not know if I can persuade her,' Camilla said doubtfully.

'Tell her it is of the utmost urgency.' His tone brooked no argument. 'If she is inclined to refuse, tell her I am asking and that it will be to her own credit and for the good of all in Diddlington.'

Even while he spoke, he was moving towards the door, his hat and gloves in hand. There was purpose and determination in every word he spoke and each step he took.

'Where are you off to, John?' Lydia enquired, following him to the front door.

'I go to fetch my father and d'Almain. I want them both there as well.'

'It will be quite a squeeze in Mrs Wardle-Penfield's carriage,' she complained.

He bent and kissed her squarely on the nose.

'They will go in the landau,' he told her. 'I will return as soon as I am able, to accompany you and your aunt. Wait for me.'

'Of course.'

She was able to say no more, for he was already half-way to the street, his final words being flung over his shoulder as he went. With long, quick strides he sped up the street while she stood looking after him in some consternation. Yet she did not doubt for a moment that he had solved the riddle of the two murders, and that the Frenchman was saved.

Aunt Camilla was pulling on her bonnet, her face creased with worry.

'I am afraid, Lydia,' she said, her fingers trembling as she took her niece's hand.

'Do not worry, Aunt,' Lydia answered her confidently. 'All will be well.'

CHAPTER TWENTY-TWO

A VERY PALPABLE HIT

Mrs Wardle-Penfield was surprisingly quick to accede to their request. She said that if John asked for it, there was no question but that it must be a matter of importance. He was not one to deal with trifles. Lydia had never liked her so well as she did in that moment. However, there was no time to waste upon idle thanks. They must be going, and so the horses were harnessed and the carriage prepared with unprecedented speed.

Despite their haste, it was almost an hour before they drew up in front of Aunt Camilla's cottage to wait for John. At least he did not prove dilatory, but arrived a mere five minutes later, in the famous landau with his father and d'Almain. Lawrence Cummings, an employee at the inn and one whom Mr Thomas Savidge had deputized and had quitted himself well against the smugglers in what was now referred to by the locals as 'The Battle of Wickham

Wood', was also present, riding one of the horses from the inn's stables.

As promised, John shared the carriage with the two ladies. It was a silent trio, as if each were afraid to speak. For her part, Lydia felt some premonition of danger, which was a sensation unfamiliar enough to induce quietness. She suspected that her aunt simply did not know what to say, and considered it best to leave her as she was. As for John, she knew him well enough to be sure that he would tell her all she needed to know at the proper time.

Their pace was brisk but not excessive, and it was perhaps forty minutes before they reached the drive at Bellefleur. Several faces appeared at the windows to witness their arrival, for such a party had not paid a visit to the great house in many a year.

The two women and four men marched up the two steps to the front door, leaving their conveyances and cattle standing on the drive. John's father, being the most senior and official member of their group, knocked loudly. It needed only three raps before the door was opened and Mrs Chalfont herself stood frowning at them all.

'What is the meaning of this, Mr Savidge?' she enquired in her best mock-patrician manner.

'We are here to see Sir Hector,' John answered, giving her back look for look.

The housekeeper's face was as hard and impenetrable as the sandstone around her. 'I am sure you are aware that such a request is impossible to grant,' she said.

'It is not a request, ma'am,' John's father spoke now. 'We are going up.'

Mrs Chalfont remained very firmly planted where she stood, blocking their entry like a tree planted by the waters.

'I think,' she replied, not obviously impressed, 'that you had best return to town. We are not prepared to receive visitors today.'

She would have closed the door, but John's booted foot prevented this.

'I hope you do not mean to refuse us entry,' he said, dangerously quiet. 'I do not wish to use a lady roughly, but I will do so if I must.'

'What do you mean by this, sir?'

This objection was not voiced by Mrs Chalfont, but by Mr Tweedy. He must have been lurking in the hall behind the housekeeper, and now pushed forward to assist the lady.

'I have no quarrel with you, Tweedy,' John's father said evenly. 'At least not yet. We are here to see Sir Hector, and will not be put off. If you have nothing to hide, you have nothing to fear.'

The valet looked from father to son, filling the doorway, and appeared to make up his mind.

'You had better let the gentlemen in, Martha,' he said.

Mrs Chalfont hesitated for a moment, but apparently came to the inevitable conclusion that resistance was useless. She stepped back reluctantly and allowed the unwelcome guests to enter. They all pressed forward. First the two Savidges crossed the threshold, followed by Camilla and the Frenchman. Lydia trailed behind them, with Mr Cummings bringing up the rear.

'We shall go up now,' John repeated his father's phrase,

adding, 'and you'd best come with us, d'Almain. We may need your assistance.'

'What about me, sir?' Mr Cummings asked, clearly annoyed at being left out.

'You,' John informed him with a slight smile, 'will stay below and keep Mrs Chalfont company.'

'I think it best if I go ahead and prepare Sir Hector for your arrival,' the housekeeper said, moving forward.

'No.' John stretched out a large hand and laid hold of the lady's arm, halting her progress. 'I think not.'

'Don't let her out of your sight, Cummings,' Mr Savidge said.

'I do not understand . . .' Mr Tweedy muttered, his gaze moving from John to Mrs Chalfont.

'No,' John said again. 'I truly believe that you do not.'

'Perhaps,' Mrs Chalfont suggested, her bosom rising and falling rather markedly, 'Mr Tweedy can go and prepare Sir Hector.'

'Tweedy can come with us,' the innkeeper allowed. 'But he'd best keep his mouth shut.'

'I am coming too,' Lydia insisted. She did not know what they expected to find above stairs, but it did not sound at all pleasant, and so she added, 'You had better stay here, Aunt.'

'Yes,' Camilla agreed faintly, her nerves already near to breaking. 'But do not be long, I pray you.'

'This should not take many minutes,' John reassured her, and started up the stairs.

They all ascended in a close cluster, moving quickly and steadily.

'You really should have permitted Mrs Chalfont to go ahead,' Mr Tweedy said, swallowing so noticeably that even Lydia, several steps behind him, could not fail to perceive it. He had seemed almost menacing on her previous visit, but now she saw that although he might be dour, he was more fearful than fearsome.

'If I were a fool,' John said to him. 'And I would advise you, sir, to say nothing more until this business is finished and done with.'

They marched onward across the upstairs landing and down a long hallway until they reached a solid oak doorway. Here there was the briefest pause before John placed his hand upon the door handle, turned it, and flung the door open unceremoniously.

'What the deuce!' a muffled voice cried in the semi-gloom.

'We are come to speak with you, Sir Hector!' John called out loudly.

'How dare you . . .' the voice began again, but quickly ceased when John stepped forward, showing that he was not intimidated.

Lydia, pressing forward past the Frenchman, could clearly see a figure huddled beneath the covers in the great canopied bed. As she watched, the figure rose up with astonishing speed and agility, considering that Sir Hector was supposed to be a man of more than four-score and ten summers.

In an instant, the bed-ridden gentleman had bounded out of the other side of the bed and dashed toward the window.

'Catch him, John!' Mr Savidge shouted.

John made a valiant effort to obey his father, leaping across the now empty bed. Even d'Almain rushed forward, trying to intercept their quarry by circumnavigating the bed altogether. Only Mr Tweedy stood rooted to the spot, though whether from surprise or confusion Lydia could not tell.

In the end, it was of no avail. The man who all these weeks had hidden himself away at Bellefleur reached the window before anyone could stop him and wrenched open the heavy draperies. Just for a moment, Lydia saw him glance back at his pursuers, his face silhouetted against the sunlight now pouring into the room.

'Good God!' she cried involuntarily. 'It's Nose!'

Even as she spoke, the man drew back a pace and, with a courage born of desperation, flung himself at the closed window. There was the sharp, clear sound of glass shattering. Mr Cole dropped from view followed almost immediately by a dull thud and a loud moan.

Meanwhile, the three other men had all reached the window at almost the exact same moment and peered out after the fugitive.

'*Mon dieu!*' d'Almain cried, reverting instinctively to his native tongue.

'Not dead,' said Thomas Savidge, less dramatically.

'But I think there is very little danger that he will escape,' John concluded with grim satisfaction.

'We have him, all right.'

With that, the trio at the window turned and sauntered back toward the two who remained frozen just inside the doorway. Mr Tweedy was as pale as a mistletoe berry, Lydia thought. For herself, she was more confused than ever. The entire incident, from the instant that John opened the door until now, had taken less than a minute, but every detail was as deeply etched upon her mind as if it were a play she had seen performed a thousand times.

'John,' she croaked, her throat almost closing up in the sudden release of pent-up emotion, 'I swear that was . . . it was Mr Cole!'

'Quite right, my love.' He chuckled softly. 'And I assure you, he is not a ghost.'

'I did not think that he was.'

He placed his arm about her shoulder and led her from the room, walking just ahead of the rest. Then, as if recalled to his duties, he turned his head.

'Papa,' he said, 'you had better go and do what you can for the poor man. See if you can help him, d'Almain. I fear he may need a surgeon.'

'Surgeon!' Mr Savidge thundered. 'What he needs is the hangman.' But he accompanied the Frenchman all the same.

'This is maddening!' Lydia cried, her patience with John crumbling at last. 'I demand to know what is going on, John.'

'Never fear, sweetheart,' he answered calmly. 'I am about to reveal all.'

CHAPTER TWENTY-THREE

THE HEART OF THE MATTER

John escorted Lydia to the airy drawing-room where she had been received on her previous visit to Bellefleur. As at that time, Aunt Camilla was there with Mrs Chalfont. However, on this occasion Mrs Chalfont's arm was held firmly by Mr Cummings.

'She tried to run off, sir,' Cummings reported to John when he entered. 'Fought like a wildcat, too, but I've got her now.'

'And such language as she used . . .' Camilla was clearly scandalized.

It was only then that Lydia realized the woman's hands were tied behind her back. Her face wore a wrathful look, like some pagan goddess intent on revenge for mortal hubris.

'This is an outrage.' She almost spit the words from between her clenched teeth.

'Good job, Cummings,' was all John said to this.

'Where is Henri?' Aunt Camilla asked, seeking her beloved and not finding him.

Before John could answer, d'Almain himself appeared, along with John's father, bearing Mr Cole between them. The injured man was clearly in a great deal of pain, his face twisted and bloody from a few shards of the broken glass which had cut his left cheek and gashed his forehead.

'His leg, I think, it is broken,' the Frenchman said as they laid him on a nearby sofa.

'I've sent one of the servants for the surgeon,' Mr Savidge informed his son.

'But what does it all mean?' Aunt Camilla almost wailed, her nerves still reeling from the events of the past half-hour. 'Where is Sir Hector?'

John gave a slight cough, preparing a lengthy speech, but was forestalled by Lydia.

'If the man in the bed, whom everyone thought was Sir Hector, is really Mr Cole,' she said slowly, her eyes fixed on her betrothed, 'then I suppose we may assume that the man we thought was Mr Cole, was actually Sir Hector?'

Camilla Denton gasped. 'But that means that Sir Hector is. . . .'

'Dead.' John finished the thought which she dare not voice. 'I am afraid that you are correct.'

'I swear before God that we didn't kill him!' Cole cried out from his recumbent position.

'No?' John was not convinced. 'In that case, why were you so eager to disguise his death? Why disfigure and burn his corpse beyond recognition?'

'Do you recall, John,' Lydia asked him, 'how we

wondered, if the murderer meant to hide the identity of his victim, why he left the watch with the body?'

'Of course now it is easy to understand why,' John responded.

'Cole wanted us to identify the body as his own.'

'Several people had observed the unusual watch.' John nodded in the direction of the Frenchman. 'Monsieur d'Almain and more than one person at the Golden Cockerel among them.'

'But how did you know this?' Lydia asked him the question which was on everyone's mind.

He smiled. 'It was you and your father who provided the inspiration, my love.'

'My father and I?' She was mystified.

'Yes.' He paused, moving to stand beside the prominent fireplace like an actor mounting the stage. The other occupants of the room watched his performance in mute fascination. In addition to the party which had accompanied him, the servants were huddled together in a far corner, perhaps more horrified and confused than anyone.

'What could we possibly have said which provided the clue?' Lydia wondered aloud.

'You were speaking of your sister's probable betrothal,' he reminded her. 'You mentioned that a man of sixty was a far cry from a lover of twenty – or words to that effect.'

Lydia remembered now. It had all been a jest, something quite trivial, but in that moment John had realized that a man of more than ninety was very different also from one of fifty. Suddenly the words of poor Kate made perfect sense.

' "It wasn't his hands," ' Lydia repeated slowly.

'Precisely.' John cleared his throat once more. 'When you prodded her memory, the maid recalled that the hand which reached across to snuff out the candle that day was far too youthful to be the withered hand of Sir Hector. Unfortunately, she blurted out the truth in the presence of the valet – which sealed her fate, I'm afraid.'

All eyes turned toward Mr Tweedy, who was standing pale and round-eyed.

'I never laid a hand on Kate Eccles!' he cried defensively.

'No,' John agreed. 'But you could not resist relating what you had heard to someone else: someone who had no hesitation in killing an innocent young girl in order to further their own ends.'

The assembled company was mesmerized. They were like sailors, reeling in a storm-tossed sea, pitched from one side of the vessel to another. First their attention had been all on Mr Cole; then they were directed toward Mr Tweedy. Now there seemed to be a third party, hitherto unsuspected, and they knew not which way to look.

'What foolishness is this?' John's father demanded. 'How many murderers do we have here?'

Everyone's gaze returned to John, who leaned nonchalantly against the mantel, as cool and unruffled as ever. However, he did not answer his father's question directly.

'I think,' he said calmly, 'that we must go back to the beginning.'

The beginning, it seemed, was Sir Hector's treasure. However, when John mentioned this, he was met with almost universal derision.

'That old wives' fable!' his father scoffed.

'Some may consider it so,' John said, accepting the scepticism of his elders. 'But it was Lydia who suggested that we should, perhaps, take the tale seriously.'

'Forgive me, my boy,' Mr Savidge snorted, 'but I'm damned if I'll pay attention to the wild imaginings of a chit of a girl – even if she is to marry my son!'

'Forgive *me*, sir,' John said with a frown, 'but if Lydia could imagine the tale to be true, why should not someone else do the same? And what,' he continued, 'if that someone decided to act upon his belief – mistaken though it might be?'

'Still sounds like nonsense to me,' the older man muttered, unconvinced.

'It *was* the treasure you were after, was it not, Mrs Chalfont?' John challenged the woman, who stood silently listening.

'Nobody ever believed that old story,' she said now, in perfect command of her emotions.

'Come, come,' John chided gently. 'It is useless to dissemble at this juncture, you know. If I had any real wit, I would have wondered why, if Sir Hector was so ill, you never summoned Dr Humblebly to him. But perhaps you can explain why you placed Mr Cole here in Sir Hector's bed and passed him off as your master all these weeks?'

'Tell him, Martha,' Mr Tweedy interjected unexpectedly. 'Tell him the truth.'

'Be quiet, you fool!' the housekeeper hissed at him.

'What did she tell *you*, Tweedy?' the elder Savidge turned

on the valet.

Mr Tweedy, forced into further speech, was temporarily rendered speechless. Perhaps he was afraid of what he might reveal. Whatever the cause, he caught his lips between his teeth before continuing.

'She told me that Sir Hector had passed away one night,' he began.

'You don't have to tell these men anything, Silbert!' Mrs Chalfont cried, attempting to stop his tongue.

'The hell he doesn't!' Mr Savidge roared at her. He then turned back to the valet. 'You'd better speak willingly now, sir, or by God I'll squeeze the truth out of your lying throat with my own hands.'

Mr Tweedy cowered before his wrath, but John addressed him with more sense and less passion.

'My father will not harm you, Mr Tweedy,' he said. 'We do not need another murder in Diddlington.'

'She said she had this man here – Mr Cole – pretend to be Sir Hector for a few weeks, to try to arrange things before the new heir sold the estate from under us and we were all turned out without a reference!'

All of this tumbled from his lips in an almost incoherent rush of words, then stopped abruptly.

'And you believed that Banbury story!' Mr Savidge was almost more angry at this than at anything else he had heard so far that day.

'Why would she lie to me?' Mr Tweedy asked almost piteously. 'I – we – I thought she cared for me.'

'Paperskull,' Mr Savidge said with a snort of supreme contempt.

'But she did lie to you, sir.' John shook his head. 'It is a particularly bad habit of hers, I believe. In this instance, it was not a very good lie, but I am sure she knew how much you cared for her, and that you would be disinclined to doubt anything she said.'

'But this still does not explain how Mr Cole became involved,' Aunt Camilla complained, very sensibly.

'I do not know the precise connection between Mr Cole and Mrs Chalfont—' John said.

'I do!' Lydia broke in upon his speech, creating her own minor sensation.

'You do?' John was more curious than surprised.

'Yes,' she said. 'I only just remembered it. When we were on the stage that day, I overheard Mr Cole telling the gentleman beside him that his sister had been an actress. He was about to speak her name when the guard blew the yard of tin. I caught only the beginning. He said she was "Mrs Cha—" '

'Very careless of him,' d'Almain commented.

'No doubt he never thought that a girl would be any threat to him,' Lydia said without rancour. 'He did not even know that I was travelling to Diddlington, after all, and probably never imagined that I was paying any attention to what he said.'

The man on the sofa muttered something which sounded suspiciously like 'Hellborn witch.' However, nobody paid any heed to him, and John once more took up his own version of the tale. He surmised that Mrs Chalfont, after working at Bellefleur for some years, had written to her brother of Sir Hector's treasure. Mr Cole had seized upon the story as a possible means to easy wealth and had come down to Diddlington to see how it might be acquired.

'Why they killed the one person who could tell them where the treasure might be, I do not know,' he admitted.

'We never killed him, I tell you,' Mr Cole said with another loud groan. 'He just . . . died.'

'Harold!' his sister sought vainly to stifle what came perilously near to a confession.

'If you will assist us, sir,' John told the man on the sofa, 'I will do all that I can to see that you are transported, rather than hanged. I cannot promise the same clemency to your confederate.'

This seemed to be encouragement enough for the injured man. He probably felt that his sister was perfectly able to take care of herself. If not, and one of them had to be hanged, he certainly would prefer that it not be himself.

'We never meant him harm,' Mr Cole managed to state with considerable fortitude, considering his pain-wracked condition. 'We got him alone in his bedchamber, as planned, and tried to bully him into telling us where his treasure was hid.'

'A masterful plan,' John commented ironically.

'A waste of time,' Mr Cole confessed. 'We never got nothing out of him but Bible verses about laying up treasure in Heaven, and hiding the Word in your heart.'

'Of course!'

To everyone's consternation, this rather loud outburst escaped from the lips of Camilla Denton.

'What is it, Aunt?' Lydia asked her.

'I have just remembered . . . something,' Camilla said,

somewhat breathlessly.

'Whatever it is,' Thomas Savidge snapped irritably, 'I'm sure it can wait until we hear more from Mr Cole here.'

'O-of course,' Camilla stammered, reddening.

'Well, we had been at it for near an hour,' the malefactor resumed his narration, 'when the old man suddenly clutched at his arm, keeled over in a faint and died on us.'

'Heart couldn't take it, I suppose.' Mr Savidge shook his head sadly. 'At his age. . . .'

'Just so,' his son cut in on his speculation, then turned to Mr Cole. 'And you decided to do what you could to hide the fact that he was dead. You disfigured the body. . . .'

'Martha said it would look like it was connected with that other murder in the woods a couple of years ago,' Mr Cole supplied helpfully. 'Said it would direct suspicion away from Bellefleur and lead them all on a wild-goose chase.'

'And so it was.' John bowed slightly toward Mrs Chalfont. 'You are a clever woman, ma'am. Unfortunately, you did not count on there being another clever woman in Diddlington: namely Miss Lydia Bramwell.'

'I cannot take the credit for this,' Lydia protested.

'But for your persistence,' John reminded her, refusing to accept her modesty, 'I might not have found out about the smugglers, and realized that the two deaths were not necessarily connected. It might have ended with no more than Monsieur d'Almain being suspected, but nothing resolved.'

'But somebody would eventually have discovered that Sir Hector was not at Bellefleur,' Lydia pointed out.

'Oh,' John waved a hand, dismissing this objection, 'I have no doubt that eventually Mrs Chalfont would simply have disappeared, along with "Sir Hector". It would have been a great mystery, of course, but few would have suspected the truth.'

'But what of the treasure?' Lydia demanded.

'It may well be that there is no treasure.' John shrugged. 'Certainly these two have not discovered it.'

'How can you be sure of that?'

'Because if they had done so they would not still be here.'

'But there *is* a treasure!' Aunt Camilla stepped forward boldly. 'I am sure of it. And, what's more, I believe it to be in this very room!'

CHAPTER TWENTY-FOUR

HIDDEN IN THE HEART

There was no doubt that Camilla Denton had caught the attention of everyone present with this startling declaration. Had an artist been able to capture the scene on canvas, it would have been a dramatic moment indeed, with Camilla at the centre of a ring of faces wearing almost every possible variation of shock, surprise and disbelief.

'My dear aunt,' Lydia was the first to voice the question on everyone's mind, 'what can you mean?'

'I told you I had remembered something,' the older woman said, with a sideways glance of reproof at John's father. 'It was when Mr Cole was recounting Sir Hector's words to him. I recalled where I had heard the expression before: "Thy word have I hid in mine heart, that I might not sin against thee." '

'It sounds like something from the Old Testament,' John said slowly. 'But I do not see what it has to do with Sir Hector's treasure.'

'Perhaps not,' Aunt Camilla admitted, which did not raise the confidence of her listeners regarding her intellectual abilities. 'But I think it is curious that the vicar recently preached a sermon in connection with that very verse, and I am certain that it is the eleventh verse of the hundred-and-nineteenth Psalm!'

This pronouncement was made with an air of triumph which was lost on the assembly. They seemed quite unaware of any significance in the fact, until Lydia let out a cry and dashed over to the fireplace where John still stood looking around at the others.

'Look!' she cried, pointing to the carved heart which had attracted her attention on their previous visit. With her finger, she traced the carved letters and numbers beneath it: 'PS11911.'

' "Thy word have I hid in mine heart . . ." ' John began. *'Hid in mine heart* . . . Great God!'

Catching his breath, John reached up above the mantel and ran his fingers over the elaborate carving, feeling carefully along the edges. The others looked on in wonder, not knowing what to expect. John raised both hands, moving them feverishly across the stone.

'Aha!' he shouted suddenly and, to their amazement, lifted the great heart quite off the wall above the mantel. Immediately everyone perceived a hole in the wall behind the carving.

'The treasure!' Mr Cole almost wailed in anguish as someone else discovered that for which he had searched so long.

John laid the stone heart on the floor beside him and

reached up into the opening. Very carefully he pulled out an object which the others craned their necks in order to see. However, when he turned about to face them, all that they saw was a plain brass box. The outside was certainly unimpressive, with no carving nor any valuable inlay to proclaim its worth. Perhaps what was inside was more worth looking at, they surmised.

There did not appear to be any lock to prevent someone from reaching the prize within, so John merely lifted the lid. Standing at his shoulder, Lydia looked down at the contents, but was more mystified than ever.

'It looks like a roll of linen,' she said.

'It is a scroll of some kind,' John elucidated, slowly raising the object up in his hands.

'A map!' Mr Cole cried out. 'A treasure map.'

'No.' John shook his head, squashing that particular fantasy. 'Come here and have a look, d'Almain,' he added, motioning to the Frenchman.

Monsieur d'Almain readily obliged, squatting beside John and examining the object before him. Between them, they partially unrolled it. Lydia eyed it minutely as well.

'It is Greek to me,' she said at last, repeating Shakespeare's immortal lines.

'Quite right,' d'Almain replied, smiling. 'It is some dialect of the Greek tongue – though not Classical Greek, I'll wager.'

Meanwhile, John stood and faced them all.

'Behold Sir Hector's treasure!' he said.

'Treasure?' his father repeated with a combination of disgust and disbelief which almost exactly matched the feelings of the others. 'An old piece of parchment with some ancient Greek laundry list?'

'Oh no,' his son hastened to correct his misapprehension. 'I would wager a fairly large sum that what we hold here is a very ancient document – probably a portion of the New Testament from before the time of the Emperor Constantine.'

'*That* is the treasure!' Mr Cole subsided onto the sofa and closed his eyes as though about to breathe his last.

'That is what two people have died for so that you might possess it,' John said. 'I wonder if you think it worth the cost now?'

'I never killed anybody,' Cole muttered hopelessly.

'No.' John looked down thoughtfully at him. 'Sir Hector's death was an accident, perhaps, and I have little doubt that your sister here is responsible for Kate's murder.'

'Do you mean to say that it was Mrs Chalfont here who strangled the maid with her own hands?' his father demanded, with a glance of almost superstitious dread at the housekeeper, who still stood like a pillar of salt.

'It did not require great strength.' John shrugged. 'A woman would be quite capable of it.'

'Oh God!' Mr Tweedy's voice shook as he beheld Mrs Chalfont as though for the first time. 'Is it true, Martha? Did you. . . ?'

'Calm yourself, sir,' John told the man.

'It is my fault, then, that Kate is dead,' the poor valet said, wringing his hands, his eyes glistening with unshed tears as the enormity of it all threatened to overpower him. 'I was the one who told her – Mrs Chalfont – what I overheard the girl saying to Miss Bramwell.'

'But you did not know what she would do.' Lydia was moved to compassion by his obvious distress. 'I can scarcely conceive of it myself.'

'I always thought that Kate knew the person who killed her,' John resumed his interrupted explanation. 'The brief time span disturbed me, and there was no sign of a struggle. The housekeeper was probably on the watch for her when she left the house that morning and followed her into the garden, away from the house where they would not be seen. She probably called out to her, and Kate would not have been likely to be suspicious. When the girl turned her back, Mrs Chalfont had only to slip the cord about her neck. . . .'

'How monstrous!' Lydia exclaimed involuntarily.

'A cold-blooded crime,' d'Almain said.

'Committed by a cold-hearted woman,' Lydia continued his thought. 'And all the time, Sir Hector had told them not only where his treasure was, but also *what* it was. Yet they never understood, and probably still do not.'

'I told you that Sir Hector was a pious man. To him, this ancient manuscript was priceless.'

'I do not suppose that he ever expected to die for it,' Aunt Camilla said with a slight shudder. 'And poor Kate, too.'

'Do not forget,' John said, returning the scroll to its coffin and shutting it, 'that there was very nearly a third victim.'

'A third?' Lydia repeated.

John crossed his arms and glanced once more at the housekeeper, who turned away and looked out of the window.

'Mrs Chalfont did all she could to implicate Monsieur d'Almain in Kate's death.'

'True!' Aunt Camilla breathed and reached out for the hand of her beloved.

'She did it very well, too,' John admitted. 'She never said that she recognized the French gentleman, but only that she had seen someone who might well have been him. And yet,' he concluded flatly, 'only one of the servants had seen any strange men about – and that was several nights before, and was almost certainly Mr Cole digging in the garden for the treasure.'

'She must have known the rumours that were circulating about Monsieur d'Almain in the village,' Lydia mused aloud.

'Naturally.'

'It did not take much to fan the flames of suspicion which would condemn him.'

'And so she had no qualms about sending an innocent man to the gallows for her own crime,' Mr Savidge commented in the stern but dignified tones of His Majesty's official.

'A mere trifle,' John observed, 'considering what she had already done in the name of Mammon.'

'It is a pity,' Aunt Camilla addressed Mrs Chalfont, 'that you did not heed Sir Hector's advice to lay up treasures in Heaven rather than on earth. Had you done so, you might not now be preparing to face your Maker with the stain of murder on your conscience.'

Within the hour, all had returned to normal. The surgeon

had set Mr Cole's leg and shoulder, and he and his sister were locked up in a special room behind the stables which served as Diddlington's gaol and which had so recently been occupied by the Frenchman.

Lydia and her aunt were once more ensconced in Mrs Wardle-Penfield's old but sturdy carriage, along with John. However, on this return journey, d'Almain himself accompanied them. Each lady sat with her lover's arm about her, and with nothing remaining to dim the light of their happiness.

'I dare swear that Mrs Chalfont feels no remorse whatever for what she has done,' Lydia commented in a kind of wonder.

'Which should remind us,' d'Almain answered her, 'what a blessing guilt can be. Guilt and shame must have prevented many from acts of the most reprehensible kind. Fortunately, most of us are hampered by conscience – if not by inclination – from attending to the promptings of our baser instincts.'

'They are a wicked pair,' Camilla said, referring to the housekeeper and her brother, 'to kill for something which did not rightfully belong to them.'

'*The love of money*,' John quoted blithely, '*is the root of all evil*, as the apostle warns us.'

'Thankfully, they did not profit by their crimes,' Lydia said with some satisfaction.

'And my father has apologized to you, sir, for his unfounded suspicions.' John inclined his head in the direction of the Frenchman.

'It was only natural that, as a foreigner, I should be the

most obvious suspect.' He smiled with a somewhat rueful fatalism. 'It is my rightful role, *n'est-ce pas?*'

'Natural?' John considered the matter. 'Perhaps. But not really justifiable by any standard of reason.'

'Ah! My friend, how often is reason employed by our fellow men in such a case?'

'Very seldom, I should think,' Lydia answered his rhetorical question.

'At any rate,' d'Almain said, changing the subject, 'I must thank you both for your efforts on my behalf. Without you, I would soon be facing the prospect of a well-tied noose, rather than preparing for my wedding.'

'Though there may be little difference between the two,' John suggested.

'You will soon find out the difference for yourself, sir,' Lydia challenged him.

This directed their thoughts in more pleasant channels, and Camilla and Lydia were soon debating what might be the best dates for their prospective nuptials. The gentlemen were asked to contribute to this discussion, though it was clear that their opinion was a mere formality. This was a sphere in which ladies reigned supreme, while men were mere ciphers.

'I can hardly believe it!' Aunt Camilla said with a sigh and an adoring gaze directed toward her fiancé. 'Soon I shall be Madame d'Almain.'

Lydia and John, watching the gentleman seated opposite them, were surprised to see a flood of rose-red surge up into his cheeks. He cleared his throat, obviously ill-at-ease, and it required no great wit to discern that he was about to reveal something which caused him no little embarrassment. Even Camilla must have sensed that something was amiss.

'What is it, my dearest?' she asked apprehensively.

'There is something I must tell you, *ma chère*.' His arm tightened about her, as though he would protect her from a blow which might be of his own making.

'You are not going to confess to having killed someone?' Lydia asked him, her mind still occupied with murder and general mayhem.

The Frenchman smiled slightly before he imparted his news.

'Whatever it is,' Camilla said bravely, 'it can never change my love for you.'

'I am glad of that!' her love exclaimed, looking deep into her eyes.

'For Heaven's sake!' Lydia cried, interrupting this inappropriately intimate moment. 'Tell us what is wrong.'

'You are not going to be Madame d'Almain – precisely,' he stated simply.

'What!' Camilla blenched at this. 'You are not going to marry me?'

'Of course I am going to marry you.' He was quick to alleviate her misapprehension. 'But in truth, I am not Monsieur Henri d'Almain.'

'You are not?'

'No.' He cleared his throat again. 'I am Henri Phillipe Augustin de Bretonville, Comte d'Almain.'

'Comte d'Almain?' Camilla repeated, her mind grappling with this information but failing to comprehend its import.

'Yes. When we are wed, you will become the Comtesse d'Almain.'

'A French aristocrat.' John chuckled appreciatively. 'If that don't beat all.'

'Oh Lord!' Lydia fell into whoops, laughing until the tears streamed down her cheeks.

'How can you be so unfeeling, Lydia?' her aunt chastened her. 'This is dreadful! I cannot marry a French aristocrat.'

'You do not love me?' the horrified *comte* demanded.

'Of course I love you,' Camilla said. 'I have always loved you. But I am a mere Miss Denton, not a *comtesse!*'

'You need not fear being too grand,' d'Almain warned, realizing that her innate shyness made her feel woefully inadequate to such an exalted position. 'My title, I fear, is all that I can offer you. My family's wealth was lost in the terror.'

'But how came you into Sussex, sir?' John could not refrain from enquiring.

The *comte* explained that, while living in London he had befriended a young man whose mother had lodgings in Diddlington. Wishing to escape the narrow confines of the *émigré* community in town, and to earn his living without having to apologize for it to every aristocrat, he had moved to the country.

'I did not intend necessarily to remain in Diddlington,' he confessed charmingly, 'until I made the acquaintance of a certain Miss Denton.'

'Oh, but it is too much!' Lydia said. She had managed to govern her laughter by now. 'Forgive my unseemly behaviour, sir. But I was only thinking how Louisa's match will be thrown quite into the shade by this news. I cannot wait to write and tell Papa all about it.'

'You are incorrigible, Lydia,' her aunt said, but could not hold back a smile herself.

'If you say so, *madame la comtesse*,' her niece quizzed her. Indeed, she never afterward referred to her aunt as anything else.

With such a conclusion to a most eventful day, it was quite a gay party which descended from the carriage when it reached Fielding Place, the home of Mrs Wardle-Penfield. That good lady was on the watch for their return and invited them all in for tea. The old tabbies of the village had already begun to mew, and it was already known that something of great moment was going forward at Bellefleur that day. Naturally, the great lady of Diddlington must be assured of being the first to learn exactly what had occurred.

Mrs Wardle-Penfield was not one to be put out of countenance, but the tale unfolded by her four guests was such as to make her spill a goodly amount of tea upon her best linen – though, mercifully, not on her puce silk afternoon-dress.

'Incredible!' she cried at one point. 'Quite incredible.'

She declared that she had known all along that her French friend was too great a gentleman to have been involved in anything as sordid as murder.

'One can always tell quality, my dear *comte*.' She inclined her head graciously toward him. 'And as for that unspeakable woman and her – brother, did you say? – have I not always maintained that it was not one of our own who committed so foul a crime?'

'So you did,' Lydia agreed, exchanging a look with her aunt, which intimated their shared remembrance that the lady's suspicions had been centred almost entirely upon the Frenchman.

'Yes.' The old woman was more than pleased with herself. 'They are Londoners, you say? What else can one expect from that bastion of brutality?'

It was not long before Mrs Wardle-Penfield had pretty much talked herself into believing that she alone was responsible for solving this most perplexing problem. Had she not supplied the carriage to convey them all to the very lair of the two cowardly killers? Had it not been her sage counsel which had led to their capture?

Her visitors derived a great deal of entertainment from her performance. However, after some time, her soliloquy on the subject became too lengthy and repetitious, and everyone expressed a shocking degree of fatigue and discovered in themselves a strong necessity of being at home in order to recover from the strain of the day.

'You should be very proud of yourself,' John complimented Lydia when they were able to steal a few minutes alone together.

'I was not the one who provided the solution to this mystery,' she demurred.

'Do not be so modest, love.' He placed his hands upon her shoulders and drew her close to him. 'You know that I would never have stumbled upon the truth as I did without your help.'

'We have done well, have we not, John?' She wrapped her arms around his neck and smiled up at him.

'We are perfectly matched, I think,' he agreed.

'In that case, Mr Savidge,' she said, pouting, 'I think it most disagreeable that you have not kissed me this age.'

'That is easily remedied.'

He proceeded to rectify his omission, to their mutual satisfaction, and it was some time before he returned home to discuss the events of the past few hours with his father. His betrothed, meanwhile, made her way upstairs to her aunt's bedchamber, where the two women indulged in a comfortable coze which lasted until well after midnight. Then, feeling that quite enough had been accomplished for one day, Lydia fell into bed and into her customary deep, dreamless sleep.

CHAPTER TWENTY-FIVE

THE FINAL KNOT

Summer was at its last prayers, but managed an almost miraculous renaissance for the wedding of Miss Lydia Bramwell to Mr John Savidge. The little church was filled with the usual assembly of well-wishers, ill-wishers, and those who wished only to see and be seen. So much had transpired over the past months, that a mere wedding seemed almost insignificant in the scheme of things. Nevertheless, it represented a blessed return to the ordinary and a brief moment of gaiety and pleasure before the bleak days of autumn and winter obliterated the last of the summer roses.

Among the guests was the newly married Comte and Comtesse d'Almain, fresh from their bridal trip to the Lake District – a highly suitable corner of England for so romantic a couple. For the moment they remained at the bride's cottage, though there was already some talk that they might soon be moving nearer to town. Many eyes were upon them during the ceremony, though they had eyes for none but each other.

The bride's sister, Miss Louisa Bramwell, was there, tricked out in the very latest of London fashions, which every lady present examined with a mixture of envy and a careful catalog of each tiny detail which they might copy to embellish their own country wardrobe. Attached to Miss Bramwell's arm was her fiancé, Sir Reginald Pevensey, a dignified-looking man who must once have been quite handsome in his way. His manners were universally pleasing, though less charitable persons were inclined to dismiss him as a nincompoop. However, his future bride was clearly enamoured – if not of his person, at least of his wealth and title – and was eager to show off her 'dearest Reggie' to all and sundry. She would doubtless be as happy in their union as she had any right to expect.

Lydia was especially delighted to be once more united with her parents. It was the last time they would behold her as a spinster, and she detected an uncharacteristic mistiness in her father's eyes. Mama's expression was one of almost beatific rapture. With her youngest daughter married, and the eldest only months away from that state of ultimate felicity and security, she had fulfilled every mother's fondest dream.

Even John's father had forgotten his earlier reservations concerning his son's match. In fact, he could not have been more contented with the way that everything had turned out. Lydia might have seemed an unimpressive catch at first. However, the elevation of her relations had increased her own worth immeasurably in his eyes. Indeed, from that time on, Mr Savidge never mentioned his daughter-in-law to anyone – be they intimate friend or perfect stranger – without also taking pains to describe her sister, Lady Louisa, and her dear aunt, the Comtesse d'Almain! He had high hopes that his grandchildren would attain the loftiest of heights, quite eclipsing their humble parentage.

He had even expended a considerable amount of blunt in procuring for his offspring a wedding present beyond anything they could have imagined – or desired. Sir Hector's American relations, the new owners of Bellefleur, were not interested in cumbersome English estates, and had been eager to part with the property at an absurdly low price. Three days before their wedding, he placed the deeds in John's hands.

There was little that either John or Lydia could do but accept such a generous offer. Many of their acquaintance felt that they displayed a deplorable lack of sensibility in seeking to inhabit an aristocratic home far above the station to which they had been born. Then too, there was the fact that at least one person had been murdered there. Who could tell what supernatural baggage might encumber their new home and disturb their domestic tranquillity?

Of course, neither party cared a fig for such nonsense. John looked forward to enclosing some of the land in order to breed racehorses. Lydia expected to enjoy running a large household, and made a mental resolution to read – or at least attempt to read – every book in Bellefleur's vast library.

As for Sir Hector's famous treasure, it had by now been

identified by those who were familiar with such antiquities as perhaps the oldest extant copy of the Gospel of Saint John. There was some argument in regard to the precise date, as there always is in such cases, but the general consensus was that it was certainly no later than the beginning of the second century.

And so Lydia's season in Sussex had consequences beyond anything she could possibly have imagined. Who could blame her for the feeling of pride and self-satisfaction which filled her breast as she settled into the carriage beside her new husband and they pulled away from the inn that evening, to cheers and waves from their family and friends?

'Well, Mrs Savidge,' John quizzed her gently, 'you have had an extraordinary season, have you not?'

'I certainly have had smugglers and murderers and husbands enough for any young lady!' she retorted.

'You are content with your lot, then?'

'Reasonably so.'

'What would you add to your desiderata?' he enquired. 'Another murder, perhaps?'

'Or another husband . . .' she suggested saucily.

'I'm afraid you will have to make do with me.'

She heaved a heavy sigh. 'Very well then. It will have to be another murder.'

'I have heard of a very suspicious death in Hampshire,' he said, raising one eyebrow suggestively.

'Truly?' She was intrigued in spite of herself. 'That is not very much out of our way, is it?'

He laughed and pressed her close to his side. 'I am very

sorry, my dear,' he told her, 'but I refuse to spend the first few weeks of my married life hunting for a killer in Hampshire!'

'What better way to spend it?' she objected.

'I can think of several things I would much prefer to be doing with my new wife,' he admitted.

'What sort of things?'

'That,' he said mysteriously, 'is something which you will soon discover for yourself! I can only assure you that it will be much more pleasant, and I trust will put all thoughts of murder out of your head.'

The two Misses Digweed, watching the carriage carrying the newlyweds disappear in the distance, shook their heads and muttered their own cryptic comments, which they did not hesitate to impart to Mrs Wardle-Penfield.

'Most imprudent match,' said the eldest.

'So well-suited,' the younger added eagerly.

'A regular hoyden.'

'Charming girl.'

'It cannot last.'

'Delightful couple.'

'A pair of simpletons.'

'So clever!'

'Well, they'll rub along tolerably.'

'So they will.'